No Greater Love

To order additional copies, please contact us.
BookSurge, LLC
www.booksurge.com
1-866-308-6235
orders@booksurge.com

No Greater Love

A NOVEL

Caro Somers

2004

No Greater Love

Thanks To: My Daughter Lisa Clayton, Who Allowed Me To Use Her Poetry.

My Daughter Gina Boice, Who Inspired The Child, Lucy.

My Husband Ej Warren, Who Provided The Cover Art Work.

CHAPTER I

Visitor came infrequently. When he appeared in the doorway, Sarah beamed in recognition. The older woman slept.

"Are you keeping up with your reading?"

She pulled open a drawer and pointed to two books. One was the Watchtower. "Thy Kingdom Come Thy Will Be Done," she said triumphantly.

Visitor smiled. "Good, good."

He sat on a folding chair and surveyed the two women. Sarah, whom he had come to see, sat on the edge of the bed looking bright and attentive. She had twisted her long gray hair into a chignon held in place by tortoise shell pins. A few strands escaped from the tightly wound knot and framed her face with wispy curls, making her look like a much younger woman. Her red dress and sweater were neat and stylish and she wore soft red lipstick that outlined and defined full sensual lips. She had dark, almost black eyes that observed every-thing—sometimes with understanding, other times with pretended understanding. Visitor seemed satisfied with her appearance and let his eyes rest on the calendar above Sarah's bed.

"How old are you now, Sarah?"

She felt like a schoolgirl who suddenly knows the answer to a question and can't wait to answer. "It's getting colder."

"Yes. Yes it is," he replied. "Winter is upon us, I'm afraid."

"Thy Will Be Done," she repeated and looked to Visitor for approval.

Without comment he gestured toward the other bed. "Your roommate seems to be sleeping."

Sarah went to Florry's bed and touched her gently. "Florry, wake up!" When she got no response she shook her head sadly. "She can't hear."

"It's just as well. It's you I came to see."

Flattered at the attention, Sarah moved back to her own bed and sat on the edge as before. She cast her eyes down demurely and waited for Visitor to speak

"I came to tell —"

"My name is Sarah," she said, flashing a radiant smile.

An aide appeared in the doorway, carrying a tray that she placed on the bedside table. "HERE'S YOUR BREAKFAST, FLORRY. CAN YOU REACH IT?"

Florry replied by opening her eyes and focusing on the young woman.

"I'LL CRANK UP YOUR BED A LITTLE."

"Thank you," she said and reached for her glasses.

"DO YOU WANT YOUR HEARING AID?"

"No, it don't work so good."

"MAYBE YOU NEED A BATTERY."

Florry shrugged and drew the tray nearer.

The aide turned toward Sarah. "How about you? Are you going to the dining room or shall I bring you a tray?"

Sarah looked around the room, confused. "Where did he go?"

"There's just you and Florry. Was someone here earlier?"

"My name is Sarah," she said confidently.

The aide smiled. "You look very nice today, Sarah. Is that a new dress?"

Sarah's dark eyes twinkled and she preened like a teenager with new clothes. "My red dress," she said proudly. "My new red dress."

"It looks terrific." The aide turned to leave and said, "I'll send Abby to take you to the dining room. Okay?"

Sarah nodded even though she felt a brief moment of panic. *Abby? Is she here?*

She was walking home from a high school picnic and the sun shone and the birds sang and she was happy. Her friend Abby walked beside her.

"I think Tommie likes you," Sarah said.

Abby blushed, making her already pink skin even pinker. "Do you really think so?"

"He looks at you all the time."

"I thought he was looking at you."

"I wouldn't give him the time of day," Sarah said scornfully, tossing her dark curls.

"Would you give Joey Roberts the time of day?" she asked pointing toward a battered old Ford coming toward them.

Sarah looked up and felt the familiar rise of fear and anticipation travel through her insides until she felt weak and jittery. "Him? He makes me sick."

The car pulled over to the curb. "Hi Babes. How's my girl?" he said to Sarah, and then to Abby, "Been somewhere?"

Abby glanced at Sarah who ignored Joey like an unwanted poor relation and said cheerfully, "We've been to the senior class picnic."

"Kids' stuff! Want to go for a ride?"

"No thanks," Sarah said primly before Abby had a chance to respond. "We've got to get home."

Joey looked at her grinning roguishly. "You'll go for a ride with me someday, Miss Sarah Snooty, you can count on it." With those words he winked and sped off.

"He's such a creep. Just because he graduated a couple years ago and works in a garage he thinks he's the best thing since sliced bread." Sarah recited the words with a superior air, but her heart knew she was targeted. The thought filled her with delicious apprehension. *When the time comes, how will I deal with him?*

"Take my hand, Sarah," a pretty girl said. "I'll take you down to breakfast."

"Are you Abby?"

"Yes. And you and I are going to the dining room. Are you hungry?"

Sarah smiled and answered assertively. "Thy Will Be Done."

CHAPTER 2

"Oatmeal's cold," Florry said. "And there ain't no salt in it." She was sitting up in bed, complaining to Sarah who had just returned from breakfast.

Sarah came to her side, pulled up a chair and said, "Eat. It's good for you. Or you don't get dessert."

"What did you say?"

"No dessert," Sarah said, shaking her head and pursing her lips.

Florry sighed in disgust and reached for her hearing aid. As soon as it was in place she repeated, "What did you say?"

Sarah pondered the question, looking more like a quick and eager little bird than an old woman. "I put water on the plant."

"I told you not to do that," Florry scolded. It's a Christmas cactus and it don't want so much water."

"Yes. I know. It's going to rain."

Florry marveled at the way her roommate carried on conversations—never realizing that her replies and comments made no sense whatsoever. She appeared to be smart and 'all there' until she opened her mouth. *She ain't got no business dressing like a young girl—wearing lipstick and fancy dresses.* Disgruntled and irritated, she finished her breakfast in silence, pushed the tray away and sat on the edge of the bed. "I need to go to the bathroom, soon's I find my slippers."

Sarah bent over and placed the slippers close to the bed making Florry realize how helpful her roommate could be. "Thank you."

She reached for her walker and moved toward the open door of the adjoining bathroom. She glanced at the full length mirror and frowned at the image. *I used to be a good lookin' woman. At least that's what Ben said.* She touched the short cropped hair and decided that she looked better when she had a permanent wave. *Don't make much difference now; I look like an old lady and I don't care. Ben used to say I had a mouth made for kissin' and Lord knows we did our share of that.* The thought embarrassed her and she focused on her skin that at one time glowed with good health. *Too many wrinkles, too many years. Nobody looks good when they's ninety-five.*

As soon as Florry was inside the bathroom, Sarah began straightening the room. She meticulously folded the hand-made afghan and placed it at the foot of the bed. After pulling up the sheets and plumping the pillow, she checked Florry's bedside tray-table for scraps of paper or disposable materials. Satisfied with her work, she sat and waited.

Startled by the buzzer, Sarah jumped up and went toward the bathroom. When she opened the door, Florry said, "I need the nurse to come."

Sarah sniffed disdainfully. "You're old enough to wipe your own butt."

Florry ignored the comment and sat patiently until an aide arrived. When Florry returned to her bed, Sarah asked, "Is it time for bed?"

"No, not yet."

Sarah picked up her Watchtower book and began to read. Florry watched for a bit and then reached for her favorite stuffed animal—a fluffy white panda. She cuddled the bear until she could feel its comforting warmth. As soon as she closed her eyes, Sarah came to the bed and pulled the folded afghan up and over her face, tucking her and the bear in a cocoon-like bundle. "What are you doing?" Florry sputtered. "I can't breathe."

"Oooh, I'm so sorry." Sarah hastily peeled back the afghan and smiled shyly, begging forgiveness.

"I don't know about you Sarah. Sometimes I think you're more trouble than you're worth."

"Thy Will Be Done," she replied meekly and went back to her reading.

Florry sighed, sank down more deeply into the comforting blankets and gave way to the memories hovering just below wakefulness.

"Flor, where's my jacket?" Ben was rifling through the hall closet, impatient to leave.

"Just a minute," she said. "Got to flip these pancakes or they'll burn." Occupied at the stove, she didn't see her children smearing their fingers with margarine and dipping them into the syrup pitcher before licking them clean. Pancakes turned, she went to the closet, but not before she saw the twins' impromptu game. "Lucy, Jimmy stop that," she said over her shoulder. Holding the broad spatula in one hand she used it like a pointer to locate the missing jacket. "What do you call this?" she asked, touching the sleeve lightly.

"I thought I hung it in the back," Ben said sheepishly.

"Here it is, right in front. If it was a snake it woulda bit you," she said disgustedly.

"I thought —"

"God gave you eyes. Use 'em!"

Muttering under her breath, she hastily retrieved the almost too browned pancakes and put two on each plate. "Eat your breakfast. Bus'll be here soon and I ain't got a car to drive you to school."

Ben stood in the doorway and motioned for Florry. He held out his arms and enclosed her in a bear-like hug. "Sorry to be so stupid," he said. "I don't know what we'd do without you."

She warmed to his words of comfort and raised her head for a kiss. "It's okay. Kids are just ornery in the morning."

"I don't help much neither," he said and kissed her soundly on the lips. "Remember when we had breakfast— just the two of us? We'd read the paper and drink coffee until time for me to go to work?" Ben winked and said, "Sometimes I'd even be a little late for work—you always looked so pretty."

Florry blushed, enjoying the compliment. "I remember," she said with a trace of wistfulness, but quickly added, "Them days is gone forever." Then glancing at the children she said brusquely, "Be off with you. I'm too busy to be lollygagging."

The nine-year-old twins forking pancakes awash in syrup, were eating happily. Florry sat at the table and looked at their smeared faces and knew she was a lucky woman. *God gave me a good man and two good kids.* "Lucy! I saw you poke your brother. Quit foolin' around and eat. Clean your plate, too," she said sternly.

Lucy looked up impishly and said in her most angelic tones. "I am."

"You kids don't know what it's like to be hungry. You're spoiled."

Both children attended to the food and finished eating. Florry began collecting lunch boxes and books and hurried the twins off to wipe off their faces. In moments, she had them overcoated and laden with book bags and lunch boxes. "Be good and do what the teacher tells you. You'll get a lickin' if you don't mind, hear?"

"Yes mama," they echoed in unison.

Florry saw the knowing look they exchanged and once again observed their unspoken communication. She kissed them as they hurried through the door. "There's the bus."

Florry knew she was smiling as she rested on the bed, drifting in and out of contented euphoria.

CHAPTER 3

The medical facility where Florry and Sarah lived was county, state and federally supported and considered one of the finest in Wisconsin. The institution offered assisted living, nursing home and hospice care and had special wings for those suffering from dementia or Alzheimer's. Well-trained personnel as well as a strong ratio of caregivers to patients made for a remarkably good place to live or convalesce. Guests could come at all hours and able patients could leave at will.

Florry was aware of the first rate services of the facility and even though she would have preferred living at home, knew that she could no longer care for herself. *At least I don't have to do my own cookin' anymore.* She was waiting for lunch and looked forward to the macaroni and cheese that was on the menu. Also on the menu were canned green beans, which she did not like. *They don't taste fresh like the ones from my garden.*

She looked at her roommate. "It's Saturday and Lucy said she'd come by today."

At first, Sarah frowned at the mention of Lucy's name and then her eyes sparkled with understanding. "Yes. I know."

She went to the bedside table, opened the drawer, took out a brush and began brushing Florry's bobbed white hair, until Florry yelled. "Ouch! Don't do that. My hair don't need brushin'."

Sarah quickly dropped the brush, looking sheepish and ashamed. When she saw that Florry wasn't angry she beamed her winning smile. "Thy Kingdom Come."

"She's always fussing over me," Florry muttered under her breath.

"Who's always fussing?" said a voice from the doorway.

Florry looked up, squinted and said, "Oh it's you."

Lucy, a pleasant looking woman, laden with packages, came toward the bed and kissed her mother. Her hair, once ash blonde and now heavily streaked with gray, outlined a pretty face belying her sixty-four years. She had her mother's alert blue eyes and a wide mouth that was almost always smiling. People liked Lucy—often calling her a 'do gooder.' She never married and seemed to thrive on her 'spinster' status. "Florry's lucky to have a daughter like her," the town seniors were fond of remarking. "She sure is a good girl." Someone invariably added. "Yep, she's a good girl, all right!"

"I'm here, as advertised," Lucy said. She glanced at Sarah who watched them with great interest.

"My name is Sarah," she said as though the whole world was interested in what she had to say.

Lucy dropped her parcels on the bed, pulled up a chair and gave Sarah a big hug. "This package is for you." Sarah blinked and took the box. Lucy explained, "It's a birthday present."

"Oh?"

Sarah looked confused, so Lucy went to the bulletin board above her bed. "See the big heart? Today is your birthday and you're eighty years old!"

"Eighty?" she repeated as though the word had special meaning.

"That's right. But I must say you look really good for an eighty-year-old."

"I see." Still appearing somewhat mystified, she carefully untied the bow and unfastened the tape holding the corners of the wrapping. When the box was exposed, she folded the paper into a neat square with all the wrinkles smoothed out and wound the ribbon into a tight coil before opening the box. She removed the cover and her eyes widened in disbelief. "Candy?"

"For you. From Mom and me. Happy Birthday."

"Yes, Happy Birthday," she echoed. She held the box up to her nose and smelled deeply.

"What's wrong?" Lucy asked. "Does it smell bad?"

"Nooo," she said triumphantly. "Clean."

Lucy frowned and looked at her mother who shrugged. "Don't ask me," she mouthed.

"Why don't you try a piece and see if you like it," Lucy urged.

"No dessert," she said sadly.

Lucy gave her a permissive look. "It's okay, you can have one."

"Oookay." She popped a chocolate in her mouth looking exactly like a naughty child giving way to temptation. "Mmm."

Sarah replaced the lid and put the candy box in a drawer between two books. She examined each book carefully, chose one and took it to her easy chair where she began reading.

"I don't understand that woman," Florry complained.

"Don't talk about her when she's here in the room."

"She don't listen anyway."

"She's a good soul, Mom. You could have had a worse roommate. She looks after you."

"She should mind her own business," Florry said petulantly, but secretly felt pleased that she had an extra caregiver.

"Look how quiet she is. Reads to herself and doesn't make trouble." Lucy watched for a moment and then directed her attention to her mother. "How've you've been feeling?"

"Okay," she said sighing. "Don't have nothin' to do. I can't even read big print no more."

"I bought you big needles and some yarn. Maybe you can see well enough to crochet another afghan."

Florry rubbed her hands over her eyes, wishing that would clear the cloudiness that kept her prisoner in an ever dimming world. "Let me see what you got." She opened one of the packages and felt the nylon yarn for softness. "How much was it?"

"Don't worry, I got it on sale. Look in the other packages. There's candy —"

Florry brightened. "Candy? What kind?"

Lucy gave her a knowing smile. "I always bring the kind you like—Jordan almonds. Or don't you like them anymore?" she teased.

Florry took the box and popped one in her mouth. "I used to want these when your pa and I went to the pictures. Not that we went very often, but they cost too much for us to buy."

"Enjoy! You deserve it." Lucy produced another bag. "Look here," she said holding up a pink sweatshirt. "This is your size and best of all, it zips up the front so you won't have to pull it over your head."

Florry allowed herself to smile in admiration and then frowned. "It looks expensive."

"No, it wasn't. I promise."

"Salvation Army?"

"No, I got it at Wal-Mart. Try it on."

As she was doing that, Lucy checked the cupboard. "I'll take these dirty clothes and wash them, okay?"

Florry nodded, reveling in the feel of the downy soft sweatshirt. "Mmm, nice and warm."

Lucy stuffed her mother's laundry in a small bag, put the new purchases in a drawer and asked, "Want to go out for lunch?"

Florry was delighted. "Sure."

"I'll tell the nurse. We'll take your chair out as far as the parking lot and then you can slide into the car. I'll get your coat."

"Where are we going?"

"Hamburgers at the drive-in? That okay?"

Florry smiled in anticipation since hamburgers were her favorite food. "We never get good hamburgers in here," she complained. "They never taste right."

"I know," she agreed laughing at her mother's evaluation. "Probably healthier, but hey, hamburgers should be greasy and juicy. Right?"

Florry hastily grabbed her purse and slipped into the coat that Lucy held for her. "I'm ready."

They started down the corridor, Lucy pushing her mother past the line of patients waiting listlessly for something to happen. "Poor souls," Florry muttered under her breath.

As they neared the door, Lucy exclaimed, "Why is Sarah following us?"

Florry turned to see and shook her head in disgust. "Crazy woman."

Sarah grabbed Lucy's sleeve and exclaimed, "Don't take Florry. Don't go away."

"We're only going out for a while, Sarah. We'll be back," Lucy said soothingly.

"No! Florry can't go," she screamed at them.

An aide came to their rescue. She put an arm around Sarah's shoulder and said, "It's okay. They won't be gone long." Then she skillfully guided Sarah back toward her room. "Tell them to hurry back," she advised.

Sarah looked at her and then at the retreating figures of Lucy and Florry and said uncertainly, "Hurry back."

"That's a good girl," the aide said. "Don't worry, everything's fine."

"I see," she replied with a broad smile. "I see."

***

When Sarah got back to the room she looked askance at the mess her roommate left. She disposed of the empty bags and remade the bed with the afghan folded neatly at the foot.

She took the fluffy white panda, hugged it and returned it to its place on the shelf, between the kangaroo and brown bear. Now the room was neat once more and she could get on with her reading.

CHAPTER 4

When Lucy and her mother returned to the facility, they found Sarah lying on the floor, with arms and legs outstretched. She was counting to four as she raised first one arm, then another; one leg and then another.

"What's she doing?" Lucy asked, totally bewildered.

"It's time for her exercises," Florry said dryly.

"Really? She does exercises?"

"Every day. It must be two o'clock. Don't know how she figures that out. She don't wear a watch."

Lucy watched as Sarah continued her routine, either oblivious to their presence or ignoring them. After five sets of four counts each, she stopped and sat up. "There, all done," she said, smiling like an acrobat who has just finished an incredibly difficult routine.

She pulled herself up to a standing position using the bed for support. A look of pure wonder bathed her face. "You came back?"

Florry, sitting in her wheel chair said impatiently, "Where should I go? I live here now."

Sarah scrutinized her roommate, tilted her head to the side and asked quizzically, "Are you Florry?"

Florry shook her head from side to side, communicating her frustration to Lucy who put an arm around Sarah's shoulders. "We're back now, Sarah. You don't have to worry. Everything's okay."

"I'm so sorry," she said, flashing her beatific smile. Apparently satisfied that all was well, she sat on the edge of her bed and began to read the Watchtower. She made no sounds, but a look of complete understanding illuminated her face as she read, lips carefully forming the words.

"Let's go down the hall," Florry said. "See who's in the game room."

Lucy began to wheel her mother out of the room, when Sarah jumped up and said excitedly, "No, don't go away."

"We're not going out. Look, Mom doesn't even have her coat on."

"Oh, I see," Sarah said docilely and returned to her reading.

***

"How are you this afternoon?" Visitor asked.

Sarah looked up, startled to hear a voice. "Thy Will Be Done," she said watching his face intently.

He looked at her bulletin board before sitting opposite her. "I see that today's your birthday," he said frowning with disapproval.

At first she was delighted to have him notice, but when he continued to frown, she wanted to make amends and said brightly, "Candy, I got candy." She stood and hurriedly went to the bedside table. Visitor watched while she opened the drawer and lifted out the box of chocolates.

"You still have both books," he said, and added, "That's very good."

She nodded, happy with the compliment and anxious to share the candy. When she removed the lid and offered the box to Visitor, he became angry. "You can't have birthdays. It's forbidden. You know that, don't you Sarah?" he said sternly.

She bowed her head. Now he was angry and she didn't know what to do. Thinking for a moment, she raised her head, unsure of what to say. "My name is Sarah, and —"

She never had a chance to finish because Visitor had gone. *I didn't see him leave.* She took the box of chocolates, dropped them one by one into the wastebasket and resumed reading.

***

"Well, Mom. I've got to go now," Lucy said as she pushed the wheelchair into the room. "I'll be back in a couple of days. Anything I can bring you?"

"No. I'm fine. You could help me get into bed. I want to take a nap before they bring supper."

"Sure thing." Lucy positioned the chair near the bed; saw that her mother was comfortable and left.

Florry settled herself on the bed but remembered the birthday gift. "Sarah? Could I have a piece of chocolate?"

Sarah shook her head. "No dessert."

"Don't be so silly. Let me have a piece."

Sarah pointed to the wastebasket. "Dirty."

"What's in there? I can't see from my bed."

Sarah carried the basket to the bedside and held it for her room-mate to see. "No candy. No birthday."

Florry saw the pile of discarded chocolates and pursed her lips unable to think of anything to say. She reached for the small box on her bedside table, took out a Jordon almond and put it in her mouth. *That's okay. I like these better than chocolates, anyhow.*

CHAPTER 5

Sarah awakened early and lay very quietly, careful not to move a muscle. *Something's different.* She listened intently; separating the hallway sounds from the stillness she knew was just outside her window. Memories from the past crowded her awareness and finally she knew what was different. *It's snowing!* She sat on the edge of the bed and slipped into her robe before going to the window, conscious of cold tiles under her feet. A few tugs on the drapery cord confirmed her belief. The ground was covered with newly fallen snow glistening under the outdoor lighting. As she watched, fascinated by the fluffy white flakes floating on beams of light, she was unable to contain her delight. "Oooh, clean snow." she breathed softly.

She wanted to wake Florry, but thought she might get mad. Instead she went to the closet and took out boots that she hastily donned. They were lined with fur and she wiggled her toes in the yielding warmth. Her woolen scarf hung on a hook; she pulled it off and wrapped it around her neck. Feeling protected against the weather, she moved her easy chair nearer the window, positioning herself so that she could watch it snow.

It was mid-December and Sarah was walking home from a late band practice. She and her parents lived on the edge of town near a large field, now covered with snow. As she trudged along, she breathed deeply of the crisp night air and listened to the sound of her galoshes crunching the icy crystals. *Winter is the best time. Summer's always too hot in Wisconsin.* She heard someone following her, turned and saw that Joey was trying to stay just out of sight. He apparently realized that he was discovered and caught up to her. "Hi Babes. Where ya goin'?"

"Home, of course," she said scornfully, trying to hide her excitement.

"Wanna make snow angels?"

"Are you serious? I'm seventeen, going on eighteen. That's kid's stuff," she said, not willing to admit she still liked to make angels.

"Well, I'm gonna," Joey said as he crossed the street and slid under the barbed wire.

Sarah shook her head in disbelief and almost decided to go home when she changed her mind and followed. Joey held the wire for her and they both searched around for untrampled snow. They were beyond the town's street lights, but a full moon made it seem almost as bright as day. "Over here, Babes. This is a great spot."

Sarah was conscious of how alone she felt—in the middle of a snowy field—accompanied by a boy who both fascinated and terrified her. He pulled her to the ground and laid beside her, allowing enough room to carve out the angel's wings. The ground felt cold but the snow was light and feathery and rose in little clouds as they flailed their arms. As soon as they finished one set of angels they moved to another spot and made more, always admiring their previous attempts. "This is fun," Sarah said, before she realized that she didn't want Joey to know that she was enjoying herself.

He raced ahead and found another clean area of snow. "Over here."

She walked toward him and instinctively understood this was no longer a game. As soon as she found a fresh space, Joey lay alongside—much too close to make wings. He leaned over her and before she knew it, he was 'washing her face' with a handful of snow. "Don't," she screamed at him. "That's freezing." She started to get up but he took her wrists and pinned her down.

"Don't be in such a hurry. Let me look at ya."

She felt embarrassed and closed her eyes to block out his intense scrutiny. "Ah, c'mon. Look at me. You've got the prettiest eyes of any girl I ever seen. Black as coal and sexy too."

The word 'sexy' caused her to feel the blood rush to her face either from the frosty air or from his admiring gaze. Before she could say a word he kissed her—cold lips pressing cold lips that soon imparted warmth to her whole being. Sarah had never been kissed before. Her religion forbade dating before eighteen years of age and even then dates required chaperons. The thrill of the moment, all the more exciting because it was forbidden filled her with reckless daring. She pretended to struggle as he kissed her repeatedly, but knew that she ached for him to continue. "No," she said, mostly out of habit. "Let me go."

"I won't let you go, because you don't want me to," he said smirking in the maddening way that he had. "You like me. I know you do."

His next kiss was even more disturbing, but filled a craving deep within her. Fearful of her intense feelings, she said. "You don't know anything about me, Joey Roberts. Now let me go."

As suddenly as he restrained her wrists, he released them, jumped up and said, "Go."

Sarah was stunned at his unexpected actions and mortified by her mixed emotions. She stood, brushed the snow off her clothing, and wrapped the scarf around her neck, partially covering her mouth. As she headed across the field she heard him say. "You'll be back for more, Miss Sarah Snooty. I know you will."

On the short walk to her own home, she tried to make sense of what happened. Even now she kept the warmth of his kisses protected under the wooly scarf, delighting in the remembered feel of his lips. She hated the way he assumed that she liked him and liked to be kissed. But her heart knew she was captive and that she would refuse him nothing. The contradictory feelings were new and pristine; she saved them for further examination.

A night-light went on in the room. Sarah blinked at the unaccustomed brightness. An aide was in the doorway.

"Up so early, Sarah? It's only six o'clock."

"It's snowing."

"I know. It took me a long time to get to work. Why don't you go back to bed for a while?"

Sarah rose dutifully and went to her bed.

The aide came toward her and said, "You're wearing a scarf?" Then she glanced down at Sarah's feel and frowned. "And boots?"

Sarah shook her head in dismay. *I have to be clean and safe.* "It's snowing."

The aide smiled. "You're right, Sarah. When it's snowing you need a scarf and boots to keep you warm."

Happy to have the woman agree with her, she flashed a smile and remembered how to answer. "Yes. My name is Sarah."

***

Later that morning Lucy came, loaded with parcels stuffed into two large shopping bags. Florry looked at her daughter who seemed ready to burst with excitement. "You didn't say you were coming," and added abruptly, "Why ain't you working?"

Lucy ignored the question and blithely continued. "It's supposed to be a surprise. I've got a little tree for you and Sarah." She unpacked a miniature tree complete with tiny lights and placed it on the wide windowsill.

"You can't plug in the lights," Florry said. "They won't let us."

"Not to worry, Mom. This tree works on batteries. See?"

Sarah sat in a chair dressed in a skirt and sweater, scarf and snow boots. A look of wonderment bathed her face when the tree lights came on. "Oooh, pretty," she cooed.

She continued to watch while Lucy pulled small, brightly

wrapped boxes from her shopping bag and placed them around the tree. "These are presents for you and Sarah. And you can't open them until Christmas."

"Christmas?" Sarah repeated. She pronounced the word so slowly and fearfully that Florry wondered what was wrong.

"Ain't you never heard about Christmas?" Florry asked disgustedly.

"Thy Will Be Done," Sarah replied piously. She rose from the chair and went to her bed where she lay and stared at the ceiling.

It was then that Lucy noticed her boots and scarf. "Why do you have those on?" she asked.

Sarah's face lit up, shining with awareness. "It's snowing."

Lucy almost laughed aloud but Florry caught her eye and shook her head. "She has to wear them when it snows."

"She wears them to bed?"

"No, just in the room."

Lucy went to Sarah's side. "Let me take your boots off, Sarah. You'll get the bed dirty," she said gently.

Oh! Dirty?" She repeated 'dirty' like it was a loathsome word and visibly cringed.

"Why don't you wear your warm slippers when you're in bed and wear the boots when you walk around the room?"

Sarah beamed. "I'm so sorry." But she allowed Lucy to remove her boots and replace them with slipper sox.

"I'll leave them right by your bed, Sarah. You can put them on whenever you get up." She eyed the scarf. "Aren't you too hot with that scarf?"

"Nooo. It's snowing."

***

Sarah's eyes were closed but she knew that Visitor was in the room. He bent over her and she opened her eyes and almost smiled at him until she noticed his serious expression. When he saw that she was awake he sat down and began speaking to her. She hoped he wasn't listening to Lucy and Florry who continued chattering as though no one was there.

"I see you have some decorations."

"Yes. It's for Christmas," she said, happy that she remembered the word.

"There is no Christmas," Visitor said unsmiling.

"No?'

"No. No birthdays, no Christmas. You know that."

"Florry, it's Florry's tree," she said eager to be forgiven.

"I see. But you must not be part of it."

"Thy Kingdom Come, Thy Will Be Done," she said triumphantly.

"Good, good."

CHAPTER 6

"Deck the halls with boughs of holly," the young voices sang as they paraded through the corridors. The children stopped at every door and offered to sing a Christmas carol, sometimes off-key but with a great deal of enthusiasm. When they passed 103, Florry and Sarah's room, they peeked inside and saw that both women were awake.

One particularly attractive child, apparently the spokesperson, stepped up and said, "We can sing 'Away in a Manger.' That okay?"

Florry nodded enthusiastically as that was one of her favorites. She noticed that Sarah frowned but apparently was interested enough to sit up straighter in her easy chair.

The children crowded around the two beds and the leader began singing in a clear sweet voice, "Away in a manger." The others quickly joined, "no crib for his bed."

As she listened intently, happy that she was wearing her hearing aid, Florry wondered how many times she heard that same hymn. *I'm ninety-five so I musta heard it at least ninety times.* The thought was frightening until she remembered that she had decided not to become ninety-six.

"The little Lord Jesus laid down his sweet head." The carolers, four girls and four boys seemed incredibly young to Florry. *That one little girl reminds me of my Lucy. She had curly blonde hair and pretty blue eyes; she looked like an angel. Christmas was her favorite time of year, even more important than her birthday. As soon as we put up the tree, she'd take me aside, look at me with that little pixie smile and say, 'Let's talk about Christmas.' We'd sit on the couch and go over all the Christmas plans—who'd be coming to dinner, what she thought Santa Claus would bring . . . .* The thought was so nostalgic that Florry wiped a tear from her eye and blew her nose loudly.

"The stars in the heavens—" *Heaven? Will I go there?* Of late most of her waking hours centered on her projected death. Every morning she awakened, surprised to be alive, and questioned the teachings she had so long believed. *What if there ain't no heaven?*

"Looked down where he lay," the choristers continued, beginning to sound out of breath. Florry glanced at Sarah who appeared agitated and restless. She wanted to ask what was wrong but didn't want to interrupt the singing.

The sounds of "The little Lord Jesus," became interspersed with tearful cries of pain. All eyes were on Sarah, who was standing and screaming shrilly, "No! No Christmas!" before going to her bed and sitting there rigidly, clenching and unclenching her fists.

The children, wide-eyed and frightened, mumbled the last words, "Asleep on the hay," and hastily retreated.

Florry raised herself up in bed and reached for her walker. She went to Sarah's side and tried to comfort her roommate who began shaking and weeping hysterically. "What's wrong Sarah?"

Sarah kept repeating, "No. No Christmas," through sobbing that sometimes made her words unintelligible.

Florry sat beside her roommate and put an arm around her quivering body. After cradling her head, she felt like a mother again and found herself crooning, "It's okay, Lucy, mama's here. Don't cry." She stroked the fine gray hair that felt so much like Lucy's. *How many years have passed by since my baby sat on my lap while I brushed her hair?* The years made no difference because she would never forget Lucy's sweetness—her need to be loved. *She was a ray of sunshine in my life. Jimmy was Daddy's boy, but Lucy belonged to me.*

Florry took Sarah's hand and held it until her sobs were less violent. It had been a long time since she was able to reach out and comfort someone who was suffering. A feeling of quiet joy filled her being—a feeling that she had forgotten. Sarah looked into her eyes like a child seeking her mother's love and compassion, but when Florry saw the pain she realized that she might never know what started the outburst. *She's a good soul; too bad she's ain't 'all there.'*

An aide came into the room and stopped short when she saw

the two women, sitting side by side on the bed. "What's going on, Ladies?" she asked, sounding both amused and surprised.

"Nothin'," Florry said quickly. "Sarah and I was talking about the singers."

The aide looked at them skeptically. "I thought I heard a lot of commotion in here."

"Musta been the kids. They were noisy," Florry said off-handedly.

Sarah looked at the aide and then back at Florry. "Thy Will Be Done," she said with a radiance that seemed to light the whole room.

CHAPTER 7

On Christmas morning when Florry said they should open their presents, Sarah got a frightened look on her face. Florry shrugged and pushed Sarah's gifts aside and began to open her own. Lucy had gotten her another sweatshirt—bright red—and matched it with sweatpants. "These'll keep me warm," Florry said. "Red's my favorite color, too."

Sarah watched her unwrap a box after first shaking it. "I know what's in here," she said triumphantly. When her beloved candy appeared, she offered the box to Sarah.

Sarah shook her head. "No dessert."

"Jordon almonds ain't dessert, but suit yourself. I'll eat yours and mine, too." While she sucked on the candy, she opened two more packages. One contained handkerchiefs and the other a stuffed animal. "Look Sarah. Jimmy sent me this moose. I got ten animals now," Florry bragged. "Don't know where to put him. Ain't no more room."

Sarah went to her side, took the animal and walked around the beds, looking for space. She stopped by the window and began to stand the moose on the windowsill.

"No! Not there," Florry admonished. "Too much light will fade it. Bring it back, I'll tell you where to put it."

Sarah returned the moose and waited for instructions. "Put it on the shelf, between the monkey and the raccoon."

"I see."

When the new animal had been properly situated, Florry said, "Thank you, Sarah. Mr. Moose will be happy there."

The nurse came with morning meds and looked at the toy zoo with admiration. "How many do you have now, Florry?"

"This makes ten," she said with a great deal of pride.

"Ten? That's a lot. Do they all have names?" the nurse asked.

"Nope. They's so cute that I just like 'em around me."

"Lots of company, right?"

Warming to the subject Florry said, "You know how many I used to have?"

"I have no idea."

"Sixty! At home I had to have shelves built to hold them. They was all over the house."

"Really? What did you do with them?"

"Gave 'em to the hospital for the children's ward."

"That was nice of you. Now you don't have room for sixty. Looks like all the shelf space is filled."

"I know," Florry said, sighing deeply. "I miss 'em, though."

"I'm sure you do." She handed each lady her paper cup of pills and waited until they disappeared. "I'll see you this afternoon," she said as she left the room, pushing her cart ahead of her.

"Ain't you gonna open your Christmas presents?" Florry asked.

"No! No Christmas," Sarah said fearfully, looking around the room.

Florry wondered what she was looking for. "Ain't nobody here." The two remaining gifts were piquing Florry's curiosity and she knew she'd have to know what was inside. "Is it okay if I open them?" she asked.

Sarah nodded. "Oookay."

One of the packages came from a charitable organization that provided gifts to patients without families. Florry guessed that something knitted would be inside and she was right. "See? Here's a pair of slipper sox," she said holding them up. "Them'll keep your feet warm."

Sarah reached out for the sox and immediately put them in her drawer. Florry wondered if she was trying to hide them. She knew the second gift was purchased by Lucy, but she had no idea what the little box contained. "It's heavy. That's for sure," she told Sarah.

After untying the ribbon she removed the lid. "Oh! It's one of those snow balls. I never heard the right name for 'em." She took the sphere out of the box and held it up to the light. A beautifully dressed Victorian lady stood in the center of a park with decorated fir trees lining the perimeter. A frozen pond complete with two skating children made up the rest of the scene.

Sarah stood at her side and her face reflected awe and wonder as she peered through the glass. "Oooh, pretty," she exclaimed.

"Now watch," Florry said and turned the globe upside down. Swirls of glistening crystals clouded the little sphere and as that happened Sarah put her hand to her mouth and screamed.

"No! No! The snow—it's cold. Stop it. Stop it." She hurried over to her bed and crawled under the covers, pulling the scarf over her face.

Florry could hear her whimpering and moaning and went to her side. "It's all right. I'll put it away. You don't have to see it." She hastily got the box and when the offending snow globe was safely inside, stuffed it into her drawer, "It's all gone," she said soothingly. "You can look now."

Sarah peered out from under the scarf, her eyes darting to all the corners of the room. When she was satisfied that the gift was nowhere in sight, she sat up on the bed. "Snow?"

"Nope. All gone."

Sarah's smiled, her eyes lighting up and her face glowing with understanding. "I see."

The gift exchange and the encounter with Sarah tired Florry. "They's too much excitement around here," she said wearily. "I'm going to take a little nap."

"Oookay," Sarah said approvingly.

As soon as Florry closed her eyes the memories crowded in, vying for attention. *So many Christmases. They all run together after a while. But this is my last one here. Do they have Christmas in heaven?*

As she drifted in and out of her relaxed state she recalled one particularly sad Christmas. She was twelve at the time—too old for dolls her mother said and not old enough to get a job. She and her family lived poorly, on the edge of dire poverty. There was never enough money for any extras; sometimes supper consisted of bread and milk. "Be thankful for that," her mother told any of the five children who complained.

As the oldest, she worked alongside her mother doing all the tasks involved in keeping a large family functioning. Her father, a coal miner, made barely enough money for the seven of them. Florry could not remember a Christmas when she felt the joy and spirit of giving that Christmas was supposed to provide. All the children hung their stockings near the coal stove and on Christmas morning were pleased if they got an orange, some Brazil nuts they called 'nigger toes,' a handful of hard candy and a ginger cookie. She never remembered any of her siblings receiving pieces of coal that her mother used as incentives to behave.

Several months before Christmas, she did odd jobs for neighbors in addition to helping her mother and had saved seventy-five cents. She saw a doll at Woolworth's that she knew was meant to be hers. A few days before Christmas she showed her mother the cache of nickels and dimes and told her how she was going to spend it.

"You'll do no such thing. I can buy two pounds of ground meat with seventy-five cents. You're a big girl now. You don't need toys anymore. Give me that money."

On Christmas morning, in addition to the stocking, Florry received a pair of panties. She rolled them up with some worn underwear, an old shirt and a hair ribbon to define the head and body until she had a somewhat human form. That bundle stayed with her until she got married, always by her side at night, always ready for cuddling.

The memory of that Christmas—now fading into the twilight of her life still caused her grief. She tried to put it out of mind, but felt hot tears welling to the surface.

Sarah was bending over her, offering tissues. "Florry?" she said hesitantly. "Are you sick?"

Florry took the tissues and wiped her face, still sniffling. "No. I'm okay. I want to take a nap. Could you get my panda?"

CHAPTER 8

A few days after Christmas while Florry was sleeping, Sarah remembered what she had to do. For a long time she worried about a problem that seemed to be unsolvable. She took a hand mirror from the bedside table drawer and placed it on the floor. Then she removed her underpants and stood over the mirror.

"I can't see what's wrong," she muttered. Thinking that her dress was blocking the light she took the mirror and went to her easy chair. Checking to make sure that Florry was still asleep, she sat on the chair and pulled her dress up above her hips and slid her panties down. Then she carefully placed the mirror between her legs and tried to see. *I know there's a cut. I can't see it, but I can feel it. I got it when . . .*

She was so engrossed in examining herself that she didn't hear an aide come into the room. "What are you doing, Sarah?"

Sarah hastily put down her dress and dropped the mirror. She was embarrassed to tell the woman what she believed and said "Nothing."

The aide frowned and pursued her questioning. "Is there something wrong? Did you hurt yourself?"

"No."

"Why did you have the mirror between your legs?"

Sarah felt ashamed, but was sure that her injury would get worse if she didn't confide in someone. She beckoned for the woman to come closer and then whispered in her ear. "I have a cut."

"Is it bleeding?"

"Bleeding?" The word was familiar. *Yes, it means blood.* "No," she said firmly. "No."

"Let's go over to your bed, so that I can see," the aide said gently.

Sarah did as she was told, slipped off her boots and laid on the bed cautiously, afraid to hear what might be wrong with her. The aide lifted her dress and asked, "Where's the cut?"

"Down there," she said, pointing to her vagina.

"I see," the aide said. "That cut doesn't hurt, does it?"

She had to think before she could answer. *Once it did . . .* She replied quickly, "No. But it won't go away."

"Now listen to me, Sarah. That's not a cut and you said it didn't hurt?" Sarah nodded. "If it were a cut it would hurt and it would bleed. That's supposed to be there so you don't have to worry."

Suddenly, a weight fell from her shoulders and she smiled her brightest smile at the aide who solved her problem. "I see. My name is Sarah."

"And you're a lovely lady, Sarah," the aide said and hugged her. "Thy Will Be Done."

Joey made his presence much more obvious after the evening they carved angels in the snow. Sometimes he would be across the street when she came out of prayer meeting, while other times he managed to be on the same bus that took her to Junior College. She didn't want to admit it, but he seemed to know her whole schedule, where she went and at what time. He never stopped to talk to her, but would pass her by with a discrete wink.

She tried to ignore him, but the fluttering deep inside made her long for a date even though it was forbidden. Joey was what her father called a heathen—not good for anything. "He'll never have two nickels to rub together," her father said. "I want you to stay away from him—away from all boys until you get married. You must remain chaste."

Sarah pondered her father's words and had only a vague idea what 'chaste' meant. In school, the biology teacher gave them basic knowledge about sex and having babies, but Sarah never quite understood how it all came about. *Where does his 'thing' go?* Too embarrassed to ask for more information and lacking graphic diagrams she felt inadequately prepared to deal with boys like Joey. She didn't dare ask her mother; she wasn't even sure that her mother knew the answers.

On a cold night in January, Sarah emerged from prayer meeting and saw Joey waiting for her. "I'll walk you home through the park," he offered.

"No! I can't go with you. My dad'll kill me."

"You have to walk home anyway. No one has to know."

She wanted to refuse, but the thrill of seeing him combined with the anticipation of what might happen, changed her mind. "Okay. But I have to hurry. My folks will be expecting me."

"I know," Joey said, grinning at her. "It's not snowing, but look at the moon—just like the one when we made angels."

The memory of that evening made her want to smile, but she continued her 'hard to get' act and simply said, "I remember."

The park just ahead of them was closed for the winter—the slides and swings reduced to steel supports. The pond, used for wading in the summer, shone with a thin glaze of ice. They walked along the circular path that led to the shelter, now boarded and locked and Joey stopped. "I have a key to the shelter. Wanna see what's inside?"

Her heart skipped a beat and she had trouble answering. "No not really."

But Joey had already turned the key in the padlock and the hasp gave way. He opened the door and beckoned her. "Come in for a minute. It's warmer in here."

She knew she was making a mistake but her curiosity about him, about what he would say or do to her far outweighed her prudence. As soon as they were both inside he shut the door and grabbed a flashlight from his pocket. He shone it around the crowded space and removed a tarp that covered the lawn chairs. As soon as he spread the tarp, he placed the still lit flashlight atop the pile of stored chairs, affording enough light to break the blackness. Without a word, he pulled her down beside him and began kissing her.

"No! We can't do this," she whimpered. "My dad —"

"It's just me and you," he said with a devilish grin on his face. He looked into her face as he fingered the top button on her coat and quickly unbuttoned each in turn until her dress was exposed.

She wasn't sure what he wanted and reminded herself that he only kissed her that night in the field. Confident that she could leave at any time, she was shocked when he reached under her dress. "What are you doing? Let me go, I want to get up."

"No you don't, Babes." His fingers were inside her panties exploring and caressing—sometime gently, other times more persistently.

She knew that she should stop him but instead welcomed his deepening probes and wondered what he was searching for. And then she knew. His finger found an open space and quickly began investigating. As he fondled her, she was caught up in the delicious pleasure of the moment and desperately wanted him to continue.

He was breathing heavily now and in the dim light, she was conscious of him unzipping and hastily removing his jeans. As soon as he pulled down her panties his warm, eager body covered hers, pressing her legs apart. Before she knew what was happening his 'thing' found her 'space' and she finally understood what had been unclear. At first there was pain, then a swelling of ecstasy filled her body and she knew this forbidden pleasure was not to be denied—not ever.

She thought they were so engaged for a long period of time and she hoped it would never end, but Joey jumped up and said, "Got to get you home."

He was so abrupt that she felt ashamed that she had given in so easily. She hastily pulled up her panties and straightened out her dress. "Joey?" She wanted him to say something to her. Tell her he loved her or at least that he liked her.

He extinguished his flashlight, replaced the tarp and opened the door that he relocked. Looking at her in the moonlight, he grinned. "Did ya like that Babes? We could do it again sometime."

She was aghast at his insensitivity and became angry. "Never! I never want to see you again, Joey Roberts!"

"So now it's Miss Sarah Snooty? You'll see me again. I promise." He patted her behind, turned and left, leaving her to walk home alone.

In her own room, she removed her panties and washed out the bloodstain in the bathroom sink. Checking to make sure that she wasn't bleeding, she reflected on her 'space' that accommodated his 'thing.' *I never did understand how that worked—until tonight. But it felt so good!*

CHAPTER 9

"Happy New Year, Ladies," the nurse said when she came around with the morning meds.

"We just got done with Christmas," Florry said. "Are you sure?"

"Absolutely. This is the last day of 2003, tomorrow will start another year."

Sarah smiled and said, "I see. No more Christmas."

"That's right. No Christmas until next year. Did you two make New Year's resolutions?"

Both women said, 'No' at the same time, with Sarah appearing confused by the question.

"Ain't no use making resolutions," Florry said. *Ain't going to be here next year anyhow.* "Them's a waste of time."

The nurse gave each of them a paper cup and waited while they swallowed the pills. She turned and left. "Enjoy the last day of the year."

Florry was sitting up in bed wishing she had something to do with her hands. "Could you get me the crochet needles and yarn?" she asked Sarah. "I think Lucy put them in the cupboard.

Sarah jumped up, found the bag and handed it to Florry. She stood and watched as Florry dumped the contents on the bed. "Oooh, pretty," she said fingering the soft pastel yarn and holding it up to her face.

"Don't! You'll get it dirty," Florry said, snatching the yarn from her.

"Dirty? Am I dirty again?"

The distraught look on Sarah's face made Florry realize that she was too sharp. "It's okay. I didn't mean it."

A broad smile, like a shaft of sunbeam bathed Sarah's face. "Thy Will Be Done."

Florry sighed and nodded at her roommate, signifying that all was well. As soon as Florry removed the label from one hank of yarn and took the needles in her hands, Sarah began a game of Solitaire. *She's a good soul. Too bad she ain't . . .*

Close work was becoming harder and harder for Florry, but over the years she had crocheted so many afghans and knitted so many mittens and scarves that her fingers no longer relied totally on her eyesight. As she began the first row of stitches, without referring to a pattern she decided this would be her last project. *I can't do this kind of work anymore and I don't want to live here day after day with nothin' to do.* She glanced at her roommate, now engrossed in her card game and envied her mobility and relatively good health. *She's still a good lookin' woman. Too bad . . .*

***

Sarah was happiest when her roommate was happy. Whenever Florry had something to do or had company Sarah felt free to entertain herself. What she liked to do best, besides reading the Watchtower was playing Solitaire. *The kings and queens and jacks are my friends. They want to be neat and clean, not grimy and messy like . . .*

Sarah looked up and her face shone with recognition. Visitor had come!

"How are you today, Sarah?" he asked without taking note of the other woman.

"I'm playing cards," she said proudly. "See?"

Visitor's voice was stern. "You must not gamble, Sarah. That is forbidden."

Her face fell and she was about to collect the cards, when Visitor said, "You may play with the cards if you don't play for money."

"Oh! I see." She smiled in thanks for his permission and returned to her game.

"What did you say?" Florry asked.

"My name is Sarah."

Florry scratched at her head. *Too bad* . . .

CHAPTER 10

A few weeks after Christmas Sarah awakened and knew from the quietness in the hall that it was very early. She had to go to the bathroom, so she reached for the bed light, turned it on and swung her legs to the floor. She adjusted her scarf, stepped into her boots and started to walk toward the door when she noticed that Florry was not in bed. *Did she go away?* Sarah felt a moment of panic until she saw her roommate lying on the floor. "Florry?" she asked, "Why are you on the floor?"

There was no answer and Sarah wondered if the floor might be more comfortable, but then said, "It's too cold to sleep down there." she admonished. Florry did not move, so she took her scarf and tucked it around Florry's neck, pulled a blanket from the bed and covered her.

After going to the bathroom, she saw that Florry had not stirred. Sarah frowned and then the full impact of seeing her roommate lying motionless terrified her. She ran to the hall and began yelling. "Come. Come help." In seconds an aide and the night nurse were in the room tending to Florry. They managed to get her back into bed and worked over her while Sarah cowered in her chair, too frightened to watch.

Sarah heard spoken words that she scarcely understood—unfamiliar words like vital signs, blood pressure and trauma. In moments Florry was lifted onto a gurney and taken away. Sarah waited until they were gone and went to her bed and adjusted the sheets and blankets until the bed looked freshly made. Then she took the white panda, cradled it in her arms and brought it to her own bed. She lay there quietly but soon her fears came to the surface and she began crying. "Florry?" she called repeatedly, but no one answered.

An aide, hearing her sobs, came into the room. "What's wrong Sarah?"

"Florry? Where's Florry?"

"We took her to the hospital. But I'm sure she'll be okay," the aide said reassuringly.

"Hospital?" *I know that word.*

"She'll be back soon. Don't worry."

Sarah nodded. "I see." As soon as the aide left, she pulled the covers over her head and thought about *hospital.*

She met Joey many times after that first night in the park's storage room. Each time, she told herself that what she was doing was wrong—that she might get pregnant—but the drive to see him was stronger than her resolve. He continued to tease and manipulate her; she knew he was crude and devious, but could not stop herself from seeing him. In March, her period was late and she spent several days tormented by the thought. She was about to tell Joey, but was saved by the welcome appearance of her cycle.

Keeping their meetings from her parents presented a real problem. They had always insisted on knowing when she would be home, where and with whom she was going. Sarah became adept at lying or as she preferred to think of it, not telling the whole truth.

She wanted Joey to propose and even hinted from time to time. He always replied, "Why spoil a good thing? Don't ya like me anymore?"

"You know I do, Joey. I just get afraid, sometimes."

"'Fraid of what? I'll protect you. You're a cute chick."

She felt herself blushing at the compliment and wanted to further explain her fears, but he looked at her with devilish impudence and said, "You're the cutest chick I ever dated. Pretty eyes, sexy mouth, but I especially like your —" Here he whispered a word in her ear, the meaning she could only surmise.

"Don't sweet talk me, Joey Roberts. You know what

I'm afraid of," she said, too ashamed to put her anxiety into words.

He looked at her, grinning all the while and said, "'Fraid I'll knock you up?"

"Oh," she said, shocked at his slang. "I never told you, but in March, I almost —"

"You were late getting the 'curse'? Is that what you're trying to say?"

She lowered her eyes and realized that he wasn't taking her seriously. "But what if?"

"Don't worry about it Babes. I know people to see," he said with a 'know-it-all' air of bravado.

Sarah was appalled at his nonchalance and put the conversation out of her mind—until May. Her period was late again and this time she vowed she would share her concerns with Joey. That evening he was going to meet her at the high school after the first half of the game. Her parents allowed her to attend basketball games, so if she left early she could easily meet her curfew. Sometimes Joey located a deserted shack or warehouse for their 'dates' but more often than not they met in his car, a practice that Sarah found extremely uncomfortable. She was happy when he suggested other options.

When the band began to play, she rushed out the door and looked for Joey. As soon as she spotted his car in the parking lot, she hurried over and got inside. She planned to wait before confiding her worries, but found herself telling him about her late period before she even said, 'Hello.'

"How late are you?" he asked casually.

Sarah heard his lack of concern, but replied grimly, "Four days."

"That ain't much." He drove two miles to the edge of town and reached for her. "Come're, Babes. I need you right now."

Her misgivings disappeared in the ardor of the moment. He had a way of making her forget everything as soon as he began possessing her body. She loved every bit of him, his brusqueness, the smell of oil under his fingernails and especially the raw desire over which he seemed to have no control.

Suddenly something went wrong. As soon as he pushed inside her, she felt moisture—not just moisture, but warm flowing wetness. Raw, cold fear welled up in her throat making it difficult to swallow. In a voice that sounded strange and irrational, she shrieked, "Stop, I'm bleeding."

He quickly backed off and even in the darkness his face reflected the panic she could not control. "What's happening? My God, there's blood all over the place—all over me!"

"Help me. I'm going to die." She tried to pull up her panties to stop the flow and became hysterical. "I'm going to die," she screamed over and over as Joey put the car in gear and roared down the dirt road.

"Don't worry. I'll take you to Emergency."

"No! What will my parents say?" But the threat of dying in Joey's car far outweighed the wrath of her parents. She closed her eyes and tried to breathe, but even that was an effort. Willing the car to go faster, she pleaded, "Hurry, please hurry."

When Joey stopped at the entrance to Emergency, she was near collapsing from shock and anxiety. *What will they do to me?* Two attendants came out and lifted her onto a gurney and before she knew it she was wheeled into a cubicle and a doctor was bending over her.

Her teeth were chattering and when she looked into the doctor's eyes, she saw genuine compassion and caring. Then he smiled, trying to ease her agitation, while he asked questions. She could make no sense of his words and let go . . .

***

Sometime later she awakened in a hospital bed and saw her mother and father watching her. They didn't say anything, but continued to stare at her, apparently waiting for her to speak. Her mother's expression was one of sadness and worry, while her father regarded her with harsh intolerance. *He hates me.* She felt disembodied—like she was floating in mid air. When she remembered everything that happened, she knew she was in grave trouble.

Finally, her mother spoke. In measured terse words, she said, "We talked to the doctor. He said you had a spontaneous abortion. He said you're going to be okay."

Her father said nothing, his lips tensed in a thin line.

"I'm sorry," she said and the tears crept into her eyes, making it hard to see.

"We'll talk when we get you home," her father said. "The doctor wants you to stay overnight—just to make sure that —"

Sarah knew that her father would not discuss anything as crass and 'female' as bleeding. She had to be thankful that she didn't need a transfusion or she may have died from loss of blood. "I'm sorry," she repeated and then turned her face toward the wall.

They tiptoed out quietly without saying goodbye. She had the rest of the night to reflect over her indiscretion. *I know I made a mistake, but I love him. It wasn't his fault. If we were married everything would be all right.* She kept those thoughts until morning when her parents arrived to take her home. They left town the next day, left no forwarding address and moved to Carson City. She never saw Joey again.

Florry's in that hospital? The nearly forgotten memories brought back the nightmare she experienced that night before escaping to a quiet place. She visualized Florry, blood stained and writhing in pain and wanted to help her. *Poor Florry!* She hastily got out of bed, put on her boots and found a clean dress in the closet. After she slipped the dress over her head and rewrapped the scarf, she took a sweater from the drawer and headed toward the lobby.

She got as far as the front desk when the night nurse looked up and said, "Sarah? Why aren't you in bed? It's very late."

Sarah considered her words. "Yes, I see." Then she remembered the hospital and the blood and began to cry.

"Let me take you back to your room."

"No! Florry's gone." The nurse didn't seem to know that she had to find her. That she had to go to her.

"Florry is fine. She went to the hospital and I'm sure she'll be back here soon."

Sarah did not believe her and wondered how she could sneak out the door and go to Florry. *She doesn't understand.* "Please. I have to go," she said and moved toward the lobby.

The nurse came around the desk and put an arm around her. "Come with me. We'll call the hospital and find out how she is."

Sarah thought the woman was trying to help so she went with her to the office telephone. She could only hear one part of the conversation, but the nurse kept smiling and saying, 'That's good, that's good.' When she hung up she accompanied Sarah to her room and sat with her on the bed.

"Florry's going to be back tomorrow. She had a bad fall, but nothing was broken. They were afraid that she might have had a stroke, but the doctor said that she just needs to come here and rest."

"No blood?" asked Sarah fearfully.

"No. She'll probably have a lot of bruises when she gets back, but that's it."

Sarah looked into her eyes and said solemnly, "I see. Thy Will Be Done."

CHAPTER 11

Florry knew she was in the hospital before she opened her eyes. As her eyesight weakened and her hearing lessened, she became more acutely aware of odors. Hospitals smelled of alcohol and sanitation and she always wondered whether they were too clean. *Ma always said we had to eat a ton of dirt before we die.*

She breathed with the help of a respirator and from the irritating tapes on her wrists and arms knew she must be hooked up to bottles of one kind or another. The sensations were not new and she added these latest aggravations to the reasons why she was so tired of living. *If they'd only leave me alone.*

Faintly she heard the comings and goings of the nurses and doctor as they periodically checked on her. She purposely kept her eyes closed because she had thinking to do and opening her eyes would make her forget the dream—if it was a dream. Pretending to be asleep might keep the attendants from talking to her.

She thought back to the previous night and remembered nothing except that she had to go to the bathroom. She was supposed to call for help—particularly when she wanted to get out of bed, but asking for help was never her choice. *I can do for myself! That's why the good Lord gave me a body.* After forming that thought, she had to smile to herself. *Body ain't much good no more.*

The dream from which she awakened bothered her and she wasn't sure she understood its meaning. It began with Ben coming to her bedside. That in itself was confusing because she buried him ten years earlier. But in the dream, he was real. And she knew he was real.

"Hey Flor, what are you doing in bed?" Ben asked. "Don't feel good?"

She laughed weakly. "I fell again. Ma always told me I was clumsy. Guess she was right."

"Are you hurt?"

"Don't think so. Probably be black and blue tomorrow."

"Well, you're going to have to be more careful." He bent down closer to her face, winked and said, "I came by to ask if you want to go fishing."

There was nothing that Florry enjoyed more than fishing, except eating the freshly caught fish. She sighed. "Don't think they'll let me go. They's not sure what's wrong with me, but I can tell 'em. I'm old."

Ben grinned at her, in the way she had come to love in their fifty-year-old marriage. "Maybe you can sneak out. I've got the truck out back. We'll go for a couple of hours and then I'll bring you right back."

The idea began to have more and more appeal. "Take a look out in the hall and see if anyone's coming. I'll try to find my clothes."

As Ben checked the corridor, Florry remembered that she had come to the hospital in pajamas. *Don't spect I can go fishin' like this.* When Ben returned, she said, "I don't have no clothes. They's at the nursing home."

"Well, you come along anyway. We'll stop by and get you something to wear."

She slid out of bed and as soon as her feet touched the floor, she was surprised at how strong she felt. *Why have I been using a walker?* Ben led the way, opening the door and guiding her toward the outside entrance. He was only a few steps ahead; when the lobby door came into view, she noticed that it was bright and sunny. *What a wonderful day to go fishin'.* She could hardly wait to get out into the welcoming light. Even Ben was illuminated in the doorframe and she felt surrounded by radiance. Then Ben stopped and turned to face her. She noticed an unusual look on his face—sadness? uncertainty? He frowned and said, "You can't come yet. It's not time." When he saw her look of dejection, added, "You got to have clothes."

"But you said we could get 'em," she pleaded. "Don't leave me here." Even as she said those words, he began walking away from her—out the door and into the brilliant sunshine. Before she could stop him he faded into the distance, glowing like a shining star.

Faintly she heard him say, "Maybe next time. I'll be back."

The outside door closed and she was left in the hall. She rubbed her eyes not sure whether she was awake or asleep. Through the window she could see it snowing, thick heavy flakes making it hard to see the parking lot. "What happened to the sun?" she muttered. "What happened to Ben?"

At that point she realized that she must have been dreaming.

"Mrs. Hendricks? Can you hear me?"

CHAPTER 12

When Lucy heard about her mother's accident—falling out of bed and then being taken to the hospital—she was furious. She came to the facility early the next morning, before Florry returned and insisted on speaking to the administrator.

"How can you allow a woman my mother's age fall out of bed?" she demanded. "Where were the bars and why weren't they in place?"

The nursing administrator listened quietly while Lucy sputtered out her wrath and indignation. "Please, Miss Hendricks, I can explain."

"I hope so, or I'm going to sue this place."

"According to law, we cannot use restraints for patients like your mother. She's lucid and capable of moving on her own."

"You what?" She had trouble believing what the woman was saying.

"We have told your mother repeatedly that she should call us whenever she wishes to get up. We are most interested in her safety and feel she should be assisted at all times. But as far as the bed bars, it's out of the question."

"Well, I never! What kind of a crazy law is that?"

"I know it sounds irresponsible but that's the way it is. Perhaps you can impress upon your mother that she should never hesitate to ask for help. We are as concerned about her safety as you are. Unfortunately she is strong willed and doesn't like to ask for assistance."

"I agree," she said ruefully, "but I have to tell you that I'm not happy with this 'no restraint' law." She sighed. "Guess I'll have to talk to Mom."

"I'm sorry she won't let us do more for her."

"Me, too. Thanks for explaining." Just before the administrator left, Lucy asked, "When will she be coming back here?"

"I think the ambulance is on the way."

"Fine. I'll wait in her room."

Lucy walked down the hall to 103 and saw that Sarah was sitting on the bed, her bedside table in front of her playing cards. When she came into the room, Sarah blinked and hurriedly gave her the news. "Florry went to the hospital," she said like she was sharing confidential information.

"That she did, but she's coming back soon."

Lucy noticed that the Solitaire hand was laid out perfectly with even spaces between the cards. Every time that Sarah dealt three cards from the deck, she always did it in the same way and placed the cards in exactly the same place. Whenever she had to add a card to the descending order, she made sure that all the others were straight with the same amount of edges showing on each card.

Lucy watched the expression on Sarah's face and couldn't help but wonder what she looked like as a younger woman. Even now, at eighty, her skin was fair and smooth with few wrinkles. She had a small nose, slightly turned up at the end giving her a elfin-like appearance. Her hair, a silvery gray was pulled back from her face, but little tendrils escaped and seemed to have a life of their own. *I'll bet she had curly hair. But her eyes are still beautiful—so dark and full of life. I wonder what goes on in that mind of hers. To look at her you'd never guess that she's senile—maybe she's just living in a different world.*

Noise out in the hall, cut short her musing and she heard her mother's voice. "This is my room," she said to the attendant, as though he needed to be instructed.

Lucy snickered. "There's mom and she sounds like she's in great form."

Florry arrived in a wheelchair and Lucy looked at her carefully. She didn't seem to be any worse for her experience. Her white hair was neatly combed and her eyes, once clear and steely blue, now somewhat dimmed, acknowledged Lucy's presence. "What are you doing here? Why aren't you working?"

"I came to see you. They called me last night and I was going to go to the hospital, but they said you were okay and that I should come today. I can only stay for a few minutes, but I wanted to check on you."

"Well, you didn't need to bother," she said impudently. "I just fell out of bed."

"Why didn't you press your 'call' button?"

"I ain't helpless, you know. I can still get out of bed on my own."

Lucy looked at her mother skeptically, but the look was lost on her. *She's going to be a stubborn old lady until she dies. There's no getting around it.* "Mom, listen to me. I just talked to an administrator and she told me that it's against the law to put bars on your bed. What they want you to do is call them instead of getting up on your own."

"Humph."

My words are falling on deaf ears! The irony of the truism almost made her laugh and she wanted to share it with her mother, but realized her mother would never understand. Instead she said, "Will you promise me that you won't try this again?" Florry nodded and glanced at Sarah. "She found me on the floor and called the nurse.

"You're lucky to have her or you might still be lying on that floor."

Sarah looked from one to the other, trying to follow the conversation. Then her face lit up in recognition. "Are you Lucy?"

"Yes, I am. And I'll bet your name is Sarah?"

Her dark eyes grew wide in wonderment and she grinned like a child being discovered. "Yes. It's going to snow."

Florry shrugged her shoulders, pointed to her head and made circular motions with her finger. "She ain't all there," she whispered.

CHAPTER 13

Florry faced some hard truths while she was in the hospital. All her life she had only contempt for people who took their own lives. *They ain't got the right to play God. Besides Pastor says it's a sin to commit suicide.* Whenever she read news articles about assisted suicide, she took the part of the victim. *Sounds like murder to me.* Those were her feelings when she entered the nursing facility in August. Now after six months, she wasn't so sure. As her eyesight became increasingly dim and her hearing more indistinct, she wondered why she was still alive. *God should let me die; I can't do nothin' except eat and sleep—I'm like a baby. My friends are gone, Ben's been gone a long time. Lucy and Jimmy are sixty-four—old people. They don't need me no more; the government'll take care of 'em.*

Her plotting began in the hospital while she was attached to a respirator. She must have looked startled when the tubes were in place, because the nurse said, "This will help you breathe, Mrs. Hendricks." That very moment, it was as though a light switched on in her head. *If I ain't hooked up to this thing, will I die?* She was vaguely aware that the machine was run by electricity and as she thought about it, a feeling of helplessness wrapped around her like a blanket, making her wonder if she had any controls left. *I can't even get out of bed and pull the plug.*

She reviewed all the suicide methods she had read about in the past—poison, gun shot, carbon monoxide, jumping from a high place—and realized that none of these methods were available. *What's a body to do? When you're tired of living you should be able to find a way out. I don't care what Pastor says. When he gets to be ninety-five, he can tell me what to do.*

Then she had an idea. *Maybe if I stop taking all those pills. Some of them must be heart pills.* The meds nurse appeared three times daily, always carrying little paper cups neatly arranged on her cart. She always stayed in their room until they swallowed everything. *Could I keep some back in my mouth and spit them out later?* She smiled to herself and vowed to practice as soon as she got back to the facility.

She began thinking about Ben. *Was that a dream or was he really here?* She knew of stories where dying people believed a loved one would come to lead them to heaven. *Is that why he came?* Seeing him so vividly—so alive—made her realize how much she missed him. *Ten years is long enough to live alone. My friends is all gone; I'm the only one left.* She recalled that last moment before Ben slipped out of sight. 'Maybe next time. I'll be back,' he said and disappeared. The more she thought about the dream—if it was a dream—the more confused she became. *Please Lord, tell me what to do.*

The seriousness of her dilemma weighed upon her until she began weeping quietly. The respirator monitor must have alerted someone because in seconds a nurse was at her bed. She took her hand and said, "What's wrong Mrs. Hendricks? Are you in pain?"

Her manner was so gentle and caring that Florry cried even harder. She shook her head and managed to say, "No. I'm okay."

The nurse stayed at her side, speaking words of encouragement until Florry stopped crying. She patted her hand. "That's better. "I'll see if we can unhook this respirator. Sometimes they can be uncomfortable."

Florry managed a faint smile. "Thank you," she whispered. In spite of the kindness expressed by the nurse, she could only feel despair. *How can I make them understand that what I'm living now is not a life?*

CHAPTER 14

One morning an aide came into their room and announced, "It's Valentine's Day, Ladies."

Florry looked up and felt utterly dejected. *After Christmas, we have New Year's, then Valentine's Day, then Easter, then on and on and on. I'm sick of it, sick of acting like I care.* The aide seemed so eager to please that she felt compelled to ask, "What will we have to do on Valentine's Day?"

"You won't have to do anything except come to a party in the dining room. We'll have cake and ice-cream and give out Valentines."

Sarah, who was playing Solitaire said, "Valentines?" Then she formed the word silently and seemed to understand, but added solemnly, "No birthday."

"This is different," the aide explained. "It's no one's birthday, we're just going to have cake and ice-cream."

"Oh, I see." She raised her eyes and looked intently at the aide before breaking into a bright smile.

"I'll come and get you about two o'clock," the aide said cheerfully.

Florry nodded tiredly. *Everything used to be more fun. Now I eat and sleep because there's nothin' else to do.* She reached for her box of candy, chose a pink one that she believed was the most flavorful color and made herself more comfortable. As soon as she closed her eyes the past crowded in pushing away the present.

Ben held her arm tightly as they walked up the short flight of stairs to the Justice of the Peace's office. "Do you really think we should be doin' this?" she whispered. "What if somebody sees us?"

"Don't be silly Flor. You're eighteen, I'm twenty. Who's to stop us?"

"I just thought it'd be nice to have some of the family here."

"Are you kidding? If you told your ma and pa that you were going to elope, they'd be after me with a shotgun."

"Even if I ain't pregnant?" she asked slyly.

"You're a little tease, aren't you?" He took her face in his hands and kissed her. "You got the bluest eyes," he said appreciatively. "Don't know how I got myself such a good lookin' woman."

"You're just lucky," she said smiling at the compliment. She shrugged. "I spect my folks will figure out I went somewheres."

"If everything goes according to plan, we'll be on that train for Chicago in an hour. We can wire them from the Station."

Florry loved this 'take charge' guy that she was marrying and it took very little convincing for her to leave home. *My life with Ben can't be any worse than livin' with ma and pa and all those kids.*

Later, thinking back on that day, she marveled at how easy it was to get married. Produce a license, say a few words and that was that. She probably should have worried about the hard times—after all it was 1933, but her life had always been hard. Now that she had a man to look after her, she vowed to be the best wife in the world.

They boarded the train for Chicago and after three hours walked into the Station and wired her parents that she was okay and that she had married Ben Hendricks. They stayed in a hotel on the south side that cost all of seventy-five cents per night. Shabby and run down though it was, Florry walked around the small room containing a bed, wash basin, dresser and clothes cupboard and reveled in the knowledge that it was nicer than any room in her old home.

Her wedding night took her by surprise. She and Ben

were both virgins which made for a great deal of fumbling and awkward positions. When their initial encounter was over, Ben turned over and went to sleep. She laid awake and listened to his even breathing. *When I have kids, I'm going to tell them what this sex business is all about. Especially the girls. Ma sure kept this a big secret.*

In spite of her first introduction to sex, she and Ben learned very quickly how to satisfy each other. Now as she remembered their mutual pleasuring, she had to smile, wondering if she was blushing. He had a way of fondling and caressing her that made her body ache with want of him. Even now, she felt a tingling sensation deep in her loins as she imagined him entering her body.

No, I can't think of him right now! I got to find a way to join him.

"Florry? Here's your medication. I'll roll up your bed and get you some fresh water."

"Okay," she said and reached for the cup. *I'll try not to swallow.* As the nurse turned to give Sarah her pills, Florry wedged hers into the back of her mouth and hoped that she wouldn't gag. After taking a small sip of water, she forced a smile on her face and nodded to the nurse, who left the room.

The contents of her mouth went into the 'spittin' tray' as she called it and she replaced the bitter tasting pills by sucking on an almond candy. Feeling very smug and secure, she lay back on the bed and wondered how soon she would die.

CHAPTER 15

"Hello?" Lucy said after the first ring.

"This is Mrs. Kline from the Carson County Care Facility. Are you Miss Hendricks?"

Oh, oh. Something's happened to Mom. "Yes, but please call me Lucy. Is something wrong?" Even as she asked, she could feel her throat tighten.

"I don't want to alarm you, but we are a little concerned about your mother."

"Yes? Tell me," she said and clutched the phone tightly as though that would ease her fears.

"We believe your mother is depressed and —"

"Depressed? She couldn't be. I just saw her a few days ago and—"

"I understand your concern and we may be wrong but —"

"How do you know she's depressed?" Lucy asked, trying to keep the annoyance out of her voice. *They must be crazy, Mom's never been depressed.*

"We found medication in the bedside tray. The one patients use for brushing their teeth or rinsing their dentures."

"What kind of medication?" She was becoming more interested in her caller's accusations.

"We believe that your mother has decided not to swallow her pills. We think she tries to keep them in her mouth and spit them out after the nurse leaves."

"How long has this been going on?" Lucy asked, appalled at what she considered unprofessional carelessness.

Mrs. Kline was quick to answer. "Only twice."

"You actually found pills that she had not taken?"

"Yes. The first time she covered them with tissue. The aide that emptied the trays commented on a strange substance she couldn't identify. So we watched her carefully the next time and she cleverly kept the pills in her mouth until the nurse left the room. Then she spit them out."

"Why would she do that?"

"That's what we're trying to determine." Mrs. Kline paused for a moment and said in a more confidential tone. "I must tell you that sometimes patients, who have decided to die, believe that only their medication is keeping them alive. Consequently they choose not to take their pills."

Lucy sighed deeply as she began to believe Mrs. Kline's suspicions. "Did you ask her why she did this?"

"We asked and she said the medication made a bad taste in her mouth."

"I must say, this is certainly shocking. I thought Mother was doing well and seemed fairly content."

"I suspect this all started after she came home from the hospital—when she fell, I mean. A few of the aides reported that she is quieter and less friendly than she used to be. Like she's thinking of something else."

"What do you think we should do?"

"Actually that's the reason I'm calling. We'd like to have a counselor talk with your mother. We have several good therapists that we call in from time to time. With your permission —"

"Of course. Whatever you think will help. Is there anything that I can do?"

"Not at the moment. You've been good about visiting your mother. Even though you're working I notice that you come to see her at least twice a week."

"I wish I could do more. My brother lives in Denver and most of Mother's family are dead, so I'm about the only relative she has left."

"As we both know, your mother is strong-willed and assertive. I doubt that your talking to her would do any good. I think it best that you not mention our conversation. The next time you visit, see if she confides in you. And try not to be accusing or judgmental."

"I'll do my best." She paused for a moment and got an idea. "I think she needs some sort of entertainment—something to get her mind off these negative thoughts."

"I agree. That's exactly what she needs." She cleared her throat. "It's been good talking to you, Lucy. Please call if you'd like more information."

"I will, thanks."

When Lucy hung up the phone, she burst into tears. *How can she be thinking of such a thing? I love her, Jimmy loves her. She can't die and leave us without a mother.* For a while she sat and allowed the tears to flow. She couldn't understand why her mother, who had always been strong and positive, should now suddenly decide she was tired of living. *It doesn't make sense. I've got to do something to help her.*

CHAPTER 16

Lucy went to the facility two days after Mrs. Kline's call. Trying to think of a way to help her mother, she went to the library and checked out two 'Talking Books.' One dramatized Biblical events and the other was a collection of short stories. She had a small cassette player that she thought her mother could operate. Armed with the machine and tapes and two boxes of Jordan almonds, she went to the facility unannounced.

"What are you doing here?" her mother asked. "Ain't you supposed to be working? You didn't say you were coming."

Lucy laughed. "Do you realize that you say that to me every time I come? You're beginning to sound like a broken record." She dropped her shopping bag on the bed and added, "I took a little time off so that I could surprise you—you and Sarah."

At the mention of her name, Sarah looked at Lucy and said, "It's going to snow."

Lucy laughed. "I don't think so. Not today." She glanced down. "You can take your boots off—and the scarf."

"Oh, I see." She removed the scarf but left her boots on. As soon as Lucy sat near her mother's bed and began talking, Sarah pulled open the drawer and took out the deck of cards. Lucy saw two books in the drawer besides the cards and a few toilet articles. She knew that one of the books was Watchtower, but could see no title on the other. *Wonder that that one is? I've never seen her read it.*

Sarah shut the drawer and began dealing Solitaire with her customary precision. Lucy watched the exacting ritual for a moment, shook her head in bewilderment and turned her attention toward her mother.

Florry was pointing at the shopping bag. "What's that?"

"Something to help you pass the time, keep you busy," Lucy said.

Florry looked up quickly and Lucy saw that her mother was instantly wary. "I don't need to pass the time," she said angrily. "You sound like that man who came to see me —"

"Someone came to see you?"

"Yes, and I told him I didn't want people bothering me with games or things to do. I got my crocheting and that's enough. None of his business anyway."

"Maybe he was trying to be nice—see if you were happy here," Lucy said meekly.

"Fiddlesticks. I don't need nobody to be nice to me."

"Well I want you to see what I brought." Lucy took the cassette player and the tapes from her bag."

"No candy?"

"Would I forget such an important thing?" Lucy reached into the bag again and handed her two boxes of almonds. One went into the drawer alongside two other boxes, the other remained in her hand. Florry ripped open the cardboard flap and offered one to Lucy.

"No thanks. Not my favorite."

"Then I'll have one," she said. "I'd offer one to Sarah, but she always says, 'No dessert,' whatever that means."

"Getting quite a stash of candy, aren't you?" Lucy teased.

Florry pursed her lips and didn't reply. "What's this other stuff?"

"Talking Books, Mom. You can listen to stories and if you like doing that, I can get more tapes."

"Listen to stories? You know I can't hear good. I can't even see the TV up there on the wall or I'd be watching."

"I know that. That's why I thought you'd enjoy just listening to something. You can hold the recorder up close to your ear." She could see that her mother was not impressed, but tried once more to be convincing. "I think you'd really like 'Talking Books' once you try."

"I don't know how to work that thing," Florry complained.

"I'll show you." Lucy proceeded to explain which buttons to push and how to load in the cassettes.

Her mother watched, but Lucy knew she was only being polite

and appeared to have no interest. When the first tape began to play, she said, "That sounds all jumbled. What are they talking about?"

Lucy took a deep breath knowing that her mother was being obstinate. "I'll leave it here for a couple of days. If you don't want it, I'll take it back."

"Good!" Seemingly aware that she hurt Lucy's feelings she said persuasively, "I will take more candy. Sure you don't want one?"

Lucy shook her head and shrugged. "Okay. You win." She sat back in her chair and asked, "Who was the man who came to see you?"

"You mean you don't know about him?" she asked suspiciously.

"Nope. Tell me."

"He asked a bunch of dumb questions. Like I was in school or somethin'."

"What kind of questions?"

She recited each question as though it was memorized, sounding more irritated and frustrated with every word. "How are you feeling today, Mrs. Hendricks?" she began in a mimicking voice. "Tell me about your family?" she simpered, pretending to be interested. "Are you comfortable in this room?" she inquired like a hotel manager speaking to a guest. "Would you like me to bring you some books?" she entreated, smiling sweetly.

Lucy burst out laughing. "You're really something else, Mom. You should go on the stage. You sounded just like an actress giving a performance."

"You'd be mad, too if you had to listen to him," she said impatiently, but Lucy could see that even she was secretly amused by her impersonation.

"He was probably trying to be friendly."

"Friendly, my foot. He was damn nosey."

The conversation was not accomplishing anything so Lucy changed the subject. "Jimmy e-mailed me yesterday. He's going to come and see you on Mother's Day."

Florry's face lit up. "Really?" And then her face fell. "That's a long time from now."

"Not so long. Mother's Day is early this year, May 9th. Today's February the 18th. He'll be coming in less than three months." Florry was silent and Lucy could almost read her thoughts. *She thinks three months is a long time. Maybe I shouldn't have told her yet.*

"It'll be good to see him again," she said with a small measure of enthusiasm. "Will he bring Betsy? What about my granddaughter, Jerry Ann?"

"He didn't say, but I imagine all three of them will come. Jerry Ann lives in Minneapolis now, so they could all meet at O'Hare and drive up here together."

"Where will they stay?" Florry asked and Lucy knew she was thinking about her house that was sold.

"At my place, of course. They stayed with me the last time they came. Don't you remember?"

Florry passed a hand over her forehead and sighed deeply. "I remember. It's not like it used to be. The old house had plenty of room."

"That it did. But don't worry. We'll all get together. Maybe go out for dinner on Mother's Day."

"That'd be nice," Florry said listlessly and then suddenly asked, "Why are you still working? Ain't you sixty-four?"

I wonder what brought this on? "You know how old I am, Mom. I could have retired at sixty-two but this way I'll have a bigger pension when I'm sixty-five."

"Don't you have Social Security?"

"I decided to wait until next year to draw it. You get a little more that way." She scrutinized her mother's face, noting the deepened lines of worry. "I've told you all about my retirement plans and when I'd quit working. Did you forget?"

"No. I just wanted to make sure that you were taken —" She stopped abruptly and passed a hand over her forehead. "I just forgot," she said with a half smile.

"Well you don't have to worry about me. I'm fine and good old Uncle Sam will look after me in my dotage."

Seemingly satisfied, Florry smiled and said, "That's good."

Lucy had no idea what to say next and could see that her visit was not creating the effect she intended. Besides, while her mother was complaining about her male visitor, Lucy got an idea that she wanted to pursue. *I know just the person to straighten her out. Let's see how she deals with him.* "Listen, Mom, I think I'd better go. I took time from the office and I have to get back. Anything I can bring you?"

"Nope. I'm fine."

***

After Lucy left, Florry wondered how her daughter could think that three months was 'not so long'. *I ain't goin' to be here three months from now.* That thought made her sad as she realized she'd never see Jimmy again. He lived so far away that his visits were twice yearly at best. *Don't matter. I can't wait no longer.*

She thought about what means were left, now that her pill swallowing experiment had failed. *I should have spit those pills in the toilet. I have to think of somethin' else. They sure had their nerve bringing in that man to talk to me. He thought I was depressed. He don't know nothin' about me.*

CHAPTER 17

The next morning, Florry had a visitor. She heard the familiar voice and looked up from her crocheting. "Pastor Sorensen, is that you?"

"It is indeed." He was a big man, fondly called 'The Great Dane' by his congregation. When he sat in the small folding chair, the chair disappeared under his ample body. He took Florry's hand and held it for a moment all the while looking at her intently. "I must say you're looking good, Florry."

She smiled at his good humor, glad to have such an important visitor. Florry liked this man and before she came to the facility, spent many waking hours at the church, both socially and spiritually. "I'm okay. Can't see too good, can't hear too good, but I can still eat," she said saucily.

Pastor Sorensen laughed heartily and before he could say another word, Sarah jumped up from her chair, nearly hysterical. "Where did you come from?"

Pastor stood and moved toward Sarah to try and comfort her. The closer he got, the more she screamed. "No, Don't touch me —"

Florry pushed the call button and an aide came rushing into the room. "What's wrong Sarah?" she asked, putting her arm around the distraught woman.

"No!" she kept repeating while pointing at the Pastor. "He's going to —"

The aide said, "Why don't you wheel Florry into the game room where you can have a little privacy? I'll look after Sarah."

Florry hastily got out of bed and into her chair and she and her visitor left the room. She was silent until they entered the game room and found a space where they could talk. Pastor pulled up a chair and faced her. "We can chat right here."

Florry, still troubled by her roommate's actions said, "Don't know what got into her."

"Maybe I upset her. She seemed to recognize me but not as Pastor Sorensen. Whoever she thought I was scared the living daylights out of her—almost like I was going to attack her." He frowned. "But she's seen me before."

"She probably forgot who you were. She don't like men and when we get a male nurse she hides in the bathroom."

"Really? I'm sorry I frightened her."

"She ain't right in the head, you know," Florry offered. "Acts kind of crazy sometimes."

"Well, be that as it may, I'm glad to see you."

Suddenly suspicious, Florry said, "Who sent you?"

"Why should anyone send me? Can't I just come to see you?"

"You can. I just thought after that man came —"

"A man came to see you? Is this a serious situation?" the Pastor teased.

Florry knew she was blushing. "I'm too old for that."

"Do you want to tell me about the man?"

"He was a pain in the —" she stopped and put her hand over her mouth, "in the neck," she added hoping the Pastor didn't guess what she was about to say. "He had the idea that I was depressed and he wanted me to 'keep busy'."

"Are you depressed?" the Pastor asked candidly.

"Nope. Just tired."

"Tired of what?"

"Everything. There ain't nothin' to do, nothin' to wait for. I got Lucy and Jimmy and that's it."

"You have a lot to be thankful for. You're still bright and reasonably well. Compared to some of the folks in here, I'd say that you're lucky. You have a caring roommate even though she may act strangely, you have Lucy who visits you often, you have —"

Florry felt the clutching in her throat that signaled a deep seated anger welling within her and lashed out, "You don't understand. I never was sick a day in my life, never went to the hospital except when

I had the twins; I used to go fishin' with Ben; I even drove his motor-cycle; I went anywhere I wanted—livin' was good." She shook with fury and when she calmed down a bit, looked at her visitor with cold resolve. "This ain't livin' and you or nobody else can tell me it is."

The Pastor was silent. He took both of Florry's hands and enclosed them within his huge palms until she stopped shaking. He looked at her thoughtfully. "Your life and my life are gifts. We do not have the right to destroy these gifts. You have children who love you as God loves you—as I love you. Right now you're going through a period of depression that is not like the Florry that I know."

"Depression? I ain't depressed. Didn't you tell us that Heaven waits for us? Didn't you tell us that we would have a better life in heaven? That's what I want. I want to be with Ben and do all the things I used to do."

"I understand. And what you say is true. We do expect Heaven to be our final destination, but not by our own choosing. We are God's children; he looks after us; he comes for us when it's time."

Florry listened without hearing. *When he gets to be ninety-five, I'll pay more attention.*

Pastor let go of her hands and looked at her intently. "Will you think about what I've said?"

"Yes," she replied, eyes downcast.

"Join me in prayer. Our Father who art . . . . . ."

CHAPTER 18

Some minutes went by before Sarah felt comforted by the aide. The man who came into their room was that man. *I thought that he went away but he came back. It was so cold and snowy . . .*

The aide had an arm around Sarah and kept talking to her in a soothing voice even though Sarah wasn't listening. She didn't want to remember anything about him—about that night and now here he was again. *He's bad and dirty and . . .*

"Will he go?" she asked timorously.

"I'm sure he will. I thought you knew Pastor Sorensen."

"Nooo. I don't know him."

"He's a nice man," the aide said. "Maybe he reminded you of someone else."

Sarah smiled brightly. "Yes, I see."

"Would you like to take a little nap, Sarah? I'll pull down the bedspread for you."

Sarah dutifully removed her boots and curled up on the bed, snuggling more deeply into her scarf. After the aide pulled up the coverlet, she said, "Don't worry. Everything's fine."

Everything was not fine in the Claymore home after they moved. Her parents, realizing that Sarah had enough freedom to get herself pregnant, imposed a much more stringent set of house rules.

She was not allowed to go anywhere alone. Her father took her to prayer meeting and either stayed by her side or picked her up immediately after it was over. She lost the library science credits she had accrued in junior college and had to start over in Carson City. School was the only time that she was away from her parents.

Girls and boys alike avoided her; sometimes she even felt invisible. It was hard to be friendly with classmates who went to dances, games and school functions so she endured the loneliness and turned inward. Going to classes and reading became her whole life. Fortunately her parents never examined her reading material, so she was able to travel to distant lands, live the life of a beloved heroine, experience all that life had to offer—vicariously. Next to historical novels, reading poetry became her favorite form of escape. It wasn't long before she began writing verse, which allowed her to express her emotions freely.

She missed Joey intensely; just the thought of him made her body ache with raw, biting emptiness. Every night she comforted herself by clinging brazenly to her pillow, imagining him invading her body with his usual unrestrained fervor—while she shamelessly urged him to continue his assault—until she felt weak and exhausted. She looked forward to these 'nights with Joey' as she called them and found that after the experience, sleep came easily.

After she finished the two year program at the small college in Carson City, she secured a job at the local library. Here too, her father drove her to work and called for her at closing time. That she was virtually a prisoner sometimes worried her—especially when she realized that life was passing her by. *I'm twenty-one years old and once I had a lover; now, no one wants me and I'll die an old maid.*

CHAPTER 19

When Lucy got home from work the following day, she had two messages on her answering machine. One from Pastor Sorensen, the other from a Mr. Bailey. After kicking off her shoes and brewing a cup of tea, she dialed the Pastor.

"Hello? This is Lucy Hendricks. You left a message for me?"

"Yes." Without any small talk, the Pastor began. "I saw your mother yesterday."

"Thank you for going to see her. I thought maybe she'd listen to you."

"I'm not so sure about that, but I'm glad you let me know that she is having problems. Don't ever hesitate to call on me. Florry is a good friend."

"How did she seem to you?"

"She looks good and I told her so. If you hadn't said anything about her trying to withhold her medication, I would never have suspected that she might be depressed."

"My feelings exactly. I found it hard to believe that she may be looking for a way to die."

"I agree. She told me specifically that she is not depressed, just tired."

"She does seem to be more lethargic—compared to her behavior a few weeks ago."

"I asked her what she was tired of—and she told me in no uncertain terms."

"So she is depressed. I'm wondering what I can do to help her."

"I talked to her about the Christian view of life and life's blessings, but I'm sure she didn't want to hear what I had to say. I sensed that she was ignoring me."

Lucy felt baffled. *If her Pastor can't get through to her—what am I to do?* "Do you have any suggestions?"

"Yes, I do. I think you should get further counseling or therapy for your mother. She needs professional help."

Little icy fingers scraped around Lucy's insides making her cold with fear. "But how can she —?" The words would not surface.

"How can she commit suicide? I've seen people who had no other means, resort to very creative methods. For example, once I had a parishioner who quit eating."

"Can Mom do that?"

"She could, but as soon as the nurses are aware of what she is doing they'll have the doctor prescribe intravenous feeding."

"Then she doesn't have many choices, does she?"

"No. Not as long as she is in a care facility. But if she doesn't have counseling, she'll get more and more depressed, which can be a separate illness of its own."

Lucy sighed. "Did she tell you that a Mr. Bailey came to talk to her?"

The Pastor laughed. "She did. And according to her, he was a 'pain in the neck.' I'm sure that meeting wasn't very productive."

"She told me the same thing. I doubt that she'll listen to anybody. She's so set in her ways."

"It's a problem with older folks. But I think you should try again. She may like the next person better."

"I'll talk to Mrs. Kline. See if they have another therapist that we could use."

"Good. Let me hear from you. And incidentally, I'll be calling on her more often. Maybe she'll listen to what I have to say."

"Thank you."

When she hung up the phone, she was reluctant to call Mr. Bailey. *This conversation can't be any better.* After a few sips of tea, she dialed again.

"Mr. Bailey, this is Lucy Hendricks."

"Thanks for returning my call. You've had a chance to talk with your mother?"

"Yes. I'm afraid so and I apologize for her bad manners. She never was a gentle sweet lady, but now she has become crotchety and outspoken."

"Never mind. I'm used to geriatric patients. In a way, they have the right to speak their minds. They've earned it."

"That may be true, but I'm afraid your visit was wasted."

"In a sense, yes. But I do think your mother is harboring a deep resentment against life—a depression if you will. She may seek other ways to achieve what she sees as a goal."

"What do you advise?"

"Don't give up. Sometimes people take instant dislikes to one person that may or not be the case with another person. Ask Mrs. Kline to direct you to another therapist."

"Thank you for your time. I'll do that."

***

Lucy decided to call her brother Jimmy. *Maybe he has a better idea. After all, he was Mom's favorite; she might listen to him.* Allowing for the time change, she decided to have dinner and call at eight. *He should be home from work by then.*

CHAPTER 20

Besides being angry at the man who came and told her that she needed to 'keep busy,' Florry also resented Pastor Sorensen's visit. *Just because I spit out those damn pills they don't have to send everybody and his brother to talk to me.* She had been thinking very hard about her options. *I could quit eating.* She wondered how long it would take to starve to death since she'd read about people who lasted for weeks without food. *Right now food's all I care about—that and sleeping. But I might have to quit eating whether I like it or not.*

She was sitting in her wheelchair, watching it snow and thinking that it would never stop. "We sure are gettin' lots of snow this year," she said aloud.

Sarah, who was playing Solitaire, looked up. "Yes. I see."

Florry had an idea. *Sarah does everything I tell her. Maybe I could get her to help me.* The thought was worth considering. *If I only knew what to do and how to do it.* She focused on the nimble fingers, shuffling and dealing cards. *She's strong; ain't no arthritis in her hands.*

An image from the past crossed her mind. When she was little, her mother used to kill chickens with her bare hands. *She'd take a live chicken, grab it by the neck and twist it somehow until the chicken thrashed around and died. It looked so easy.* She put the scene out of her mind as quickly as it entered. *Surely they's somethin' I can do or have Sarah do.*

"Sarah, I want to talk to you," she said and waited until she had her attention.

"Ooookay," she replied and went back to her cards.

"No! Listen to me. I want to talk to you."

Sarah put the cards down, carefully centering them on the table, and focused on Florry. Her eyes opened wide with awareness and Florry hoped she might actually listen—and understand.

"I'm ninety-five years old," Florry began and noticed that Sarah nodded politely. "I'm ninety-five and I don't have nothin' else to give up."

Sarah frowned for a moment and said very softly, "I'm so sorry."

Florry sighed in frustration, but realized she had to tell some-one. "This is important, Sarah. Listen." Without waiting for a com-ment, she began. "When I got married, everythin' was good. Ben and me was healthy; the twins came along and they never gave us no trouble. We didn't have much money, but no one did them days. Then we found out that Ben was diabetic, so I had to change my way of cookin' and fix stuff that wouldn't hurt him."

"Thy Will Be Done," Sarah replied, in total agreement.

"Then I got fat because I was eatin' everything that Ben couldn't eat—like cakes and pies. Doctor said I had to give up sweets and rich food. I sure do miss desserts and ice-cream," she said nostalgically. Then remembering that Sarah was listening she continued. "After that, Ben got a heart condition and we had to be careful about him exerting himself." She paused, wondering if she was blushing at re-vealing information about their sex life.

Sarah was watching intently and Florry was encouraged by flick-ers of understanding that crept across her face with each disclosure. "But the most terrible thing I had to give up was Ben. We was friends and he left me all alone. It took me a whole year to make a new life for myself and then things got worst. I woke up one morning and I could hardly see myself in the mirror. Didn't know what was wrong, but I was so scared that I didn't tell anybody. I kept on driving my car even though I could hardly see." She swallowed to stifle a catch in her throat. "One day I had an accident and a woman nearly died because of me. Lucy took my car keys and —"

"Lucy took your keys?" Sarah asked with disbelief written all over her face.

Florry hastened to add, "It weren't her doing. The doctor said I couldn't see good enough to drive. Said I had a small stroke."

"Oooh. I'm sorry."

Suddenly angry, Florry said, "Do you know what it's like to have to wait for somebody to take you somewhere? All those years I went wherever I wanted to go." She stopped a sob by force of will and sputtered, "I hate this!"

Sarah nodded wisely, came to Florry's side and patted her hand. "I see."

"I'm sure you don't see, because I can't even explain to myself. It's like every year something gets taken away from my life—things I really liked. When I started blacking out and falling, Lucy talked me into selling the house and moving here. That was the house that Ben and I —" She had to stop for a moment so she wouldn't cry. "And now that's gone, too."

She paused to collect her thoughts and got a flash of insight. She grasped Sarah's hand and said excitedly, "Everybody thinks that the big things in life—like dying and getting divorced—make you sad, but the little things are worst."

Sarah looked at her so intelligently that she felt compelled to finish. "When you can't do anything for yourself anymore and have to wait for someone else, that's when you got enough. I can't wash my hair, cut my toenails, take a bath —" Here she could not stop a muffled cry from surfacing. "When you can't even go to the toilet on your own —" She bowed her head and was silent.

Sarah repeated one of her favorite phrases, "I'm so sorry."

Florry knew she was really talking to herself but finished. "When I first came in August, I could still walk a little, play bingo and make phone calls. Now I'm in the wheelchair when I ain't in bed."

Sarah blinked and with a sunburst smile, got the afghan and draped it around Florry's shoulders, wrapping her and the wheelchair into a neat bundle.

Florry sighed and allowed herself to be enfolded. *She can't help me. She don't understand. Nobody does.*

CHAPTER 21

"Hello Jimmy? This is Lucy."

"Lucy? Good to hear from you. What's up?"

"It's about Mom."

There was a sound of urgency in his voice when he asked, "What's wrong?"

"I think she's depressed. A nurse called and said she was spitting out her pills when she was supposed to be swallowing them."

"Really? Why would she want to do that?"

"Apparently sometimes patients believe they will die if they resist medication."

"And she was trying that?"

"Only once. They caught her the second time."

"Did she offer any explanation?"

"No. Said the pills had a bitter taste."

"So we don't know what she was planning."

"That's what we're trying to figure out. They sent a counselor to talk to her; she blew him off in no time. You know how feisty Mom can be." She heard a chuckle, but went on. "I asked Pastor if he would go and visit. When he met with her, he said she seemed to be angry and belligerent and showed no interest in what he had to say."

"What are we going to do?"

"I don't know. I can't believe that she's thinking suicide. She was always so down on people who did that."

"How can she? I mean, she's supervised and can't get out on her own. She has no means."

"That's true. Pastor said that sometimes patients choose to quit eating. But he said that doesn't work because the hospital facility starts IV feeding."

"I would never believe this about Mom if you hadn't told me."

"Pastor thinks I should request another counselor which I will do, but he warned of another problem."

"Like what?"

"He said that she might get more and more depressed which is an illness of its own"

"Do you want me to come out there? I can arrange a trip if you think it will help."

"No. I don't think so. I told her you were coming for Mother's Day and she seemed glad to hear that. But —"

"But what?"

"She said that was a long time to wait. I told her it was less than three months, but that didn't seem to make a difference."

Jimmy was silent. Lucy imagined the furrowing of his brow— the frown that was so like Florry's. "I don't know what to say. Let me talk to Betsy and I'll get back to you. Maybe we could come for Easter. It's April 11th this year."

"Or maybe her birthday?"

Jimmy didn't answer immediately, but she knew he read her implication. "You mean March 15?"

"Just a thought." *Why did I mention her birthday?*

"You're frightened aren't you?"

"I'm trying not to be. Forget coming on her birthday, Easter's fine." She was reluctant to say more and changed the subject. "I'll keep working on ideas—the facility is very helpful and caring—and let you know if we figure out a solution."

"Good. I'll be in touch after I talk to Betsy."

CHAPTER 22

Sarah partly understood what Florry was trying to tell her. Sometimes certain words made her remember—sometimes certain words made her forget. *Things were taken from my life too—just like Florry.*

While she was working at the library, she often used her lunch period to write poetry. Just being around books and people who read books was exhilarating and thoughts came easily. She customarily sat in a carrel, sandwich in one hand and pencil in the other. It was a private world that no one could take from her.

That day she was thinking about Joey who she had not seen for over two years. She had not forgotten him and believed that someday he would come for her—release her from the bondage that was her present life. Her feelings about him were always close to the surface making him a preferred subject for her writing. She began thinking about the poem that had occupied her free time for several days and removed it from her notebook. After reading the words she had written, her pencil began to move over the paper, almost without direction from her. She scribbled a few lines, scratched them out, added new words, wrote and rewrote. Finally she was satisfied enough to copy her work on a clean sheet.

"You so eloquently proclaim
That pleasure and pain are
Much the same,
But to you I say
There is no pleasure like
Pleasure denied.

In life's trilogy of choices
I see you choose
The premeditated ends
Caught in the stampede
Towards normality.
Why not retreat
To the impulsive cavern
Where untapped desires lurk.
Discard the façade
And rise with the
Wave of hysteria
You border on.
Allow the pressurized nerves
To leap out
And hurl the guarded energy
Towards something not quite as
Intense."

She smiled in pleasure at her efforts. *Not too bad. It needs a title and maybe a few word changes, but for now, it's okay.* She stuffed the completed poem in her notebook and returned to the front desk.

That evening, her father picked her up as usual and as usual was virtually silent on the short drive to their home. She hurried into the house, dropped her notebook on the hall table and hung her jacket in the closet.

As she went to retrieve her notebook, it fell to the floor with papers scattering everywhere. She began picking them up and noticed that her father was helping. He took the poem that she had been writing and began reading it. Her heart sank when she saw the scowl on his face. *What is he thinking?* Her parents had never shown the slightest interest in her school work nor in the books she brought home from the library.

"Where did you get this?" her father thundered.

"It's a poem," and added hesitantly, "I wrote it."

"This is not a poem. Poems have words that rhyme. Even I know that. This is filth. 'There is no pleasure like pleasure denied?' What does that mean?"

"It's what I believe," she said quietly.

"And you have 'untapped desires'? What are they, pray tell."

"I'm sorry Father. I can't explain."

"Well, I can. You have already sinned against the great Jehovah. Your body is no longer clean. Now you have the mind to match it."

She lowered her eyes, unable to respond.

Six months later, she married a man of her father's choosing—a good religious man without any romantic ideas regarding their sex life. On Sunday night, without fail he used her as his sex partner—neither demanding, nor attentive to her needs. The coming together lasted all of three minutes during which time she relived the pleasures of Joey and his uninhibited passion.

Sarah was thankful for one thing. Her new husband allowed her to work in the library. That and poetry kept life bearable.

CHAPTER 23

Mrs. Kline hadn't called in a week and Lucy was beginning to feel more hopeful about her mother. *Maybe we were all jumping to conclusions, trying to correct a problem that didn't exist.* Her sense of euphoria and relief didn't last long. On February 26th, she came home to find a message on her machine. "She might have good news," she told herself as she dialed.

"The doctor saw your mother today," Mrs. Kline began. He has started her on medication to raise her spirits and hopefully help her out of this depressive state."

"Is that really necessary? I was over there yesterday and she seemed like her old self."

"We believe that she hides her true feelings when you visit. All the staff who attends her have been advised to watch her actions and report any suspicious behavior or despondency and file a report. She is having more and more periods of utter silence when she keeps her eyes closed and is virtually uncommunicative."

"That's terrible! I never suspected she might be acting differently when I'm not there."

"We've started the medication and according to the doctor, should see some improvement in the next week or so."

"But what about the second counselor? Weren't you going to try once more?"

"I'm sorry to say that your mother barely set eyes on him, before she dismissed him. Wouldn't listen to a thing he said."

"I'm embarrassed and would like to apologize on her behalf. I don't know why she's so obstinate."

"Actually, if it weren't so serious, I'd say their first meeting must have been pretty amusing—at least for a bystander."

"How so?"

"According to Mr. Franks, he met with her in one of the private rooms. As soon as she saw him, she asked, very impertinently, 'Why aren't you in school?' He was taken aback by the inquiry and said that his first impulse was to laugh. But he didn't."

"What did he say?"

"He turned the tables on her and said. 'Today's a holiday. We didn't have school.'"

Lucy laughed aloud. "That poor man. He must be sorry he ever chose that profession."

"Well, the meeting went downhill from there. Your mother is a smart woman; she knew he was a good match for her, but that didn't change her attitude. She remained totally uncooperative until he finally left."

"I wonder why she referred to school. Is Mr. Franks a young man?"

"Not really. He's fully qualified and has excellent credentials. I'd say he was about forty."

"With people like my mother, forty is just a 'spring chicken.' I'm sorry this second meeting backfired. Guess we have to hope the pills work."

"We'll keep you informed."

"Thanks."

CHAPTER 24

When the breakfast tray came the next morning, Florry could hardly wait to eat. Her stomach had been growling for the past half hour and since it was Saturday, she hoped for something better than oatmeal. The coffee smelled good and after removing the plastic cover from the plate of food, she was delighted to see pancakes. *Mmm. They look like the ones I used to make.* She proceeded to butter the cakes and poured syrup over them. Just as she was about to put the first bite in her mouth, she remembered her plan. She looked at the steaming plate of food with mixed emotions. The odors of maple syrup and melting butter were tempting. *What shall I do? I'm hungry, but I shouldn't eat.* There were two pancakes on the dish; she decided to eat only one.

Later, when the aide came for her tray she asked if something was wrong. "You didn't eat much, Florry," she said.

"I got full. They's pretty rich."

The aide looked at her skeptically and wrote something on a card before she left the room. Florry suspected it had something to do with the pancakes. *I can't do nothin' around here but what someone notices.* She was still hungry so she ate Jordon almonds, one after another until she felt sleepy. When she lay back on the bed and closed her eyes, Sarah, who had just returned from the dining room, came to her side and covered her.

"Leave me alone," she said irritably. "I want to sleep."

Sarah drew back and then, face shining with compassion, removed her scarf and carefully wrapped it around Florry's neck.

Florry sighed and turned her head away allowing the past to envelop her.

It was Christmas and Florry was preparing a huge meal. Jimmy was off with his father while Lucy sat on a high kitchen stool watching her.

"When will the turkey be done?' Lucy asked expectantly.

"Not for an hour. Gives me time to fix the potatoes."

"Mashed? And gravy?"

"Yep, just for you, sweetie."

"Can I help do something?"

Florry looked at her ten year old daughter, admiring the ash blond hair that curled around her face like a shining cap. Lucy's blue eyes were questioning—begging to be of help. "You can set the table. Get the good dishes out of the sideboard. Grandma and grandpa will be coming."

Lucy slid off the stool and went to the dining room. "Do we need small dishes?"

"Yes. Bring those glass salad plates out here and I'll serve up the Jello. Just before we eat you can put one on each plate." While Lucy got the table ready, Florry peeled the potatoes, checked the green bean casserole and un-molded the Jello loaf. *Thank goodness, it came right out of the pan.*

Lucy came in with salad plates and 'ooed' over the Jello. "Looks pretty Mom."

"It does, if I say so myself. Nothing like red, white and green ribbon Jello for Christmas dinner. Everybody likes it, too."

"I don't," Lucy said.

"I thought you did."

"It's okay," Lucy said wrinkling her nose, "but I like mashed potatoes and gravy better."

Florry loved cooking big dinners—not only for herself but for a chance to see the pleasure that holiday meals brought her family. *Especially Lucy. That child dotes on Christmas—ever since she was a baby. Ain't nothin' more important to her—not even Halloween.*

"Here are your pills, ladies," the morning meds nurse said brightly.

Florry was irritated—not so much by the nurse's appearance, but by the fact that her daydream was interrupted. She took the paper cup and noticed an extra pill. "What's this?" she asked crossly.

"Doctor's orders."

"What for? Ain't I taking enough pills?"

"This will make you feel better—not so tired."

"I feel fine," Florry said stubbornly. "And I ain't tired."

The nurse laughed. "Take it anyway. You can talk to the Doctor next time he visits."

Florry knew or at least suspected that the new pill had something to do with her 'depression' that she so flatly denied. *If they'd only leave me alone.* She thought back to her breakfast tray and realized that unless she disposed of some of the food in the toilet, the girl bringing the tray would mark her chart. *They's all checking on me. I can't fool 'em.*

CHAPTER 25

Sometime before dawn, Florry awakened and wondered what time it was. She glanced at Sarah who seemed to be sleeping. As she started to reach for the 'call' button, she got an idea. *If I go to the bathroom myself, I might fall. I could be there for a long time before anyone finds me. I might even die.* She carefully swung her legs over the side of the bed and reached for her walker. It was just beyond her finger tips and she stretched to grab it. That's when she slid down the side of the bed and landed on the floor. Then she remembered that the reason she woke up was to pee. Now she was on the floor and couldn't get up, Sarah was asleep and she still had to pee.

She decided to relieve herself then and there which made her more comfortable, but now her night clothes were wet and the floor was hard and felt like ice. *I guess I'll just have to lay here and freeze to death.* She tried to think pleasant thoughts and ignore her shivering but the more she vowed to endure her predicament, the colder she became. *Guess this wasn't such a good idea, after all.*

She lay there for what seemed like hours. *Don't the nurses ever check on us? Maybe if I scooch up a little I can reach the button.* As she inched slowly toward the bed, Sarah sat up and said, "Florry? Is that you?"

"Of course it's me. Who do you think?"

Sarah hurriedly got out of bed and went into the hall where she began calling frantically. "Help. Help Florry."

In seconds a nurse and an aide came to 103 and the two of them got Florry back into bed. The aide went for clean pajamas and called the housekeeper to mop the floor. Sarah watched them from her chair and Florry could see that she was frightened.

"Hospital?" Sarah asked fearfully.

"No, I think she's okay. She just slipped." She smiled at Sarah. "I'm glad you called us. She could have been there for a long time."

"I see."

"I'll check her blood pressure and take her temp but I think she'll be fine. You can go back to bed."

Sarah dutifully returned to her bed and lay there quietly, watching her roommate. The aide came with clean pajamas and helped her dress. When she saw that Florry was comfortable and covered, she turned off the light. "Good night, ladies."

As soon as everyone left the room Florry raised up on one elbow. "Why did you have to call for help?" she said angrily.

"You were on the floor."

"Maybe I wanted to be on the floor. Next time leave me there," she admonished. "You're always fussing over me."

Sarah made no comment.

***

Visitor came in quietly, but Sarah knew he was in the room and hoped that he wouldn't disturb Florry. She started to sit up in bed so that she could talk to him, but he motioned her back.

"You did a strange thing a while ago," he began.

"Nooo. I just called because Florry —"

"Florry doesn't want you to call."

Sarah did not understand Visitor. *Why can't I call?* "She was cold and —"

"She doesn't want you to call," he repeated sternly.

"Oh, I see."

"You must not interfere."

Sarah felt a relieved of a great burden. "Thy Will Be Done."

Visitor left.

***

Later that morning, Lucy stormed into the room, furious with her mother. "Why are you doing this?" she said. "You know you're supposed to call for help when you want to get up."

Florry pursed her lips and ignored the question. "You don't have to run over here every time they call you. I'm okay. Didn't even get bruised."

"That's not the point. The nurses call me whenever you do anything that you're not supposed to do. They worry about you and so do I."

"Ain't no need to worry," she said and then asked her usual question. "Why ain't you working?"

"It's Saturday, in case you haven't noticed. Even lowly secretaries like me get Saturdays off."

"You make a fuss over nothin'. I just slipped. That's all."

Lucy sighed and wondered how she could impress upon her mother the seriousness of her actions. She tried a different tack. "What if you fall and no one notices—not even Sarah. You could have a heart attack and there you'd be." An enigmatic smile crossed her mother's face. *Is that what she's hoping for?* Lucy felt a chill come over her and swallowed hard before continuing. She took her mother's hands. "Listen to me. I need my mother to be safe. I can't be worrying over you all the time. I want you to be comfortable—want you to be here for me." She stifled a choke. "For me and for Jimmy. We love you, Mom."

Florry looked into her eyes and Lucy read the weariness and despair. "I know you do," she said.meekly. "I'm sorry to cause you worry."

"Okay. Let's forget about it for now." She remembered what she had come to tell her mother. "Jimmy called last night and guess what? He's coming for your birthday."

Florry looked up and Lucy could see she was pleased. "Really? March 15th?"

"Almost. March 15th is a Monday, so he and Betsy and Jerry Ann are coming on the preceding Friday or Saturday. They'll have to leave on Sunday evening."

As quickly as the expression of pleasure crossed her mother's face, it disappeared. "It'll be good to see them again," she said dutifully.

Lucy wondered what her mother was thinking. "You'll be ninety-six. Can you believe that?"

"I can believe it. I feel every minute of it some days," she said thoughtfully. "Some days I feel even older."

"That's nonsense. You look great for your age." The words of praise did not impress her mother, so she added, "What would you like for your birthday?"

Florry stared at a spot over her head. "What I want you can't give."

Lucy thought she was teasing and said, "Try me."

Florry shrugged. "Don't want nothin' that I don't have already. A birthday is like any other day—it comes and it goes."

Lucy felt distressed at the conversation and decided to leave. "I have to go, Mom. I'm meeting one of my co-workers for lunch, but before I go I want you to promise me that you'll take care of yourself." She scrutinized her mother's face before adding, "I think you know what I mean."

"I will. I will."

***

On the way home, Lucy stopped at a roadside park, put her head down on the steering wheel and gave way to waves of frustrating sobs that racked her body. *Mom wants to die and I don't know how to stop her.*

CHAPTER 26

After Lucy left that morning, Sarah had time to think. Visitor was angry with her, Lucy was angry with Florry and Florry was angry with her. She had no idea why everyone was so upset. She had always been frightened of anger—first from her father and later from her husband, Jonathon. *He wasn't as bad as father, but sometimes he scared me.* From the beginning of their marriage, Jonathon had wanted children. He and Sarah never discussed the issue of children—whether they would have a family and if they did, how many. But Sarah knew her own feelings. *I only want Joey's baby. If we had gotten married I might have had another chance.* Determined not to get pregnant, she sought information from library books. By painstaking research she found that careful douching gave her a chance to avoid pregnancy. It was in her favor that Jonathon turned over and went to sleep immediately after taking his pleasure. So every Sunday night, lights went on in their bathroom as Sarah practiced all the cleansing and preventive measures she'd read.

Occasionally, Jonathon berated her for her seeming infertility. He was never verbally mean, but she sensed a deep felt anger within him. As the years went by without once missing her period, she credited her bareness to the fact that Sunday was the Sabbath and not a day for procreation.

Besides not producing a baby, another time that she felt the brunt of Jonathon's anger was when she entered and won a poetry contest.

She had been working at the library for almost seventeen years, the last fifteen married to Jonathon. Working and reading and writing poetry kept her happy in a loveless marriage. The times that she thought Joey would come back to her were fewer and farther between. She found that it was hard to remember his face—hard to remember the feel of him. At one time she wondered whether she should go back to her hometown just to see if he was still there, but decided that she couldn't bear it if he were married and had a family of his own.

The library sponsored a poetry contest; the winner would receive a $200 prize, be published in the local paper and have a copy laminated and hung in the library with an appropriate brass marker. Sarah had many poems to choose from but decided to write one especially for this event. When it won, she was delighted and amazed and honored. Her husband felt differently.

"How can you put your name on such drivel? What does it mean?"

Sarah shook her head impatiently. "Let me read it to you. Poetry is meant to be read aloud."

She began reading, caressing the words that she had so carefully joined to express her thoughts.

"YESTERDAY
I remember a shop in Roseville
Where they sold poems
In tomato soup cans.
You could buy them
For a smile,
A kind word
Or a piece of your childhood.
The poems came in yellow and green,
But sometimes
If you told the man
About your soul
He would give you a purple one.
The purple ones were special,
But they had no meaning
Unless you believed in yourself.

The shop was closed yesterday.
The yellow and green poems
Were sold
To Sears for $1.98,
But the purple ones
Were thrown away."

Jonathon looked at her askance. "Where in the hell is this 'shop in Roseville?' There's no Roseville in Wisconsin."

"I just made it up. It could be any town—even Carson City."

"I'm telling you this for your own good Sarah; no one's ever heard of poems in tomato soup cans, either. That's nonsense!"

She tried to explain. "I was thinking of that new artist—Andy Warhol—who paints tomato soup cans. That's where I got the idea."

"He paints soup cans? Why?"

"I don't know. Maybe because no one else ever did. It's just a metaphor." She shrugged. "Why does that make you so angry?"

"I'm angry because my wife's poem will be in the paper and bandied all over town. It's disgraceful to my name," he fumed. And after warming to the subject, he added, "Don't really make much difference, though. My name will end with me. All because of you."

She bowed her head and said nothing. With the prize money, she bought a bus ticket to her old hometown, intending to find her lover. After making numerous inquiries, she found that he had died in the Korean conflict. She returned to Carson City and realized that her life would never get any better. *But it can't get any worse either, so I'll have to make do.*

As her dreams of being rescued finally came to an end, she allowed herself to become more and more involved with books, flights of fancy and abstract thinking. The world she was creating was comfortable and safe and isolated from Jonathan.

CHAPTER 27

Florry was becoming increasingly anxious about her wish not to have a ninety-sixth birthday. Spitting out pills didn't work, avoiding food was too hard and falling on the floor didn't produce the result she hoped for. *That was Sarah's fault.* As she let her mind wander, trying to invent something she could do to herself she got a bright idea.

Florry remembered the day when her favorite grocery store revamped their produce case. Florry was delighted to see plastic bags replace the brown paper ones. "Look what the A & P just did," she said to Ben when she got home.

Ben looked up from his paper. "What did they do that could get you so excited?"

"Plastic bags. And you know what? I can reuse them for other things."

Ben took one of the bags. "Did you read this? 'Warning: Keep this bag away from babies and children. Do not use in cribs, beds, carriages or playpens.'" He chuckled. "No problem for us. Jimmy and Lucy are way past that stage."

"Thank the good Lord that we managed to raise them to age twenty; we don't need to worry anymore. Let me see that bag. Why do you suppose you have to keep them away from kids?"

"The bag says, 'The thin film may cling to nose and mouth and prevent breathing.' It could suffocate you, I reckon."

"Well, I won't let that happen. But I sure do like 'em; they'll be handy."

Why didn't I think of this a long time ago? I've got all kinds of plastic bags. All I need to do is find the right time—a time when Sarah's asleep.

***

Florry had her chance a few nights later. She waited until after the night meds nurse came and waited even longer until she was sure that Sarah was asleep. There were several bags in the drawer; Lucy always left a few extra so that she could put toiletries in them. She took one and held it up to the light. *If they's a warning label, I can't read it with my eyes.* As she thought about it, she stifled a laugh at the irony. *I can't see to read so I don't know they's dangerous.*

She examined the bag carefully and judged that her head would fit inside. When she tried to open it, the plastic stuck to itself and she had to crinkle the opening several times before it opened. As she was slipping the bag over her hair and face she had second thoughts. *Do I really want to do this?* It took her one second to decide. *I'm ready.*

As the bag slipped down over her eyes and nose, she remembered the warning that Ben had read so long ago. *It really does cling to your nose and mouth.* When the bag was in place, she immediately felt closed in and snug, like being wrapped in soft, smooth silk. She told herself that this was what suffocating felt like. *It won't be so bad.* She lay back and tried to relax and think pleasant thoughts. Seconds later she began to see black spots before her eyes and her lungs felt ready to explode.

She and Ben were still newlyweds and they were sitting on the edge of the town swimming pool. Ben playfully pushed her into the water and she felt instant terror as water rushed into her nose and mouth and she began to choke. She wanted to scream that she couldn't breathe, but she had no breath to do so. She clawed the water frantically, sure that she would die and then she felt Ben's strong arms pulling her to safety.

"I didn't know you couldn't swim," he said. "I'm sorry."

After she finished coughing, she said wryly, "I thought maybe you wanted to do me in."

"I was going to, but I figured you didn't have a big enough insurance policy."

His words were facetious but she heard the remorse. "Well, just don't do it again," she said gently.

"We're going to teach you to swim—that's for sure," he said seriously. "When we go fishing I don't want to worry about you falling in the water."

As that memory faded into blackness, she had one thought. *I can't do this.* She tore at the bag, ripping it with a fingernail. "Oh, my God," she gasped. "This is too scary."

CHAPTER 28

On the eighth of March, Pastor Sorensen came again. He walked into the room slowly, apparently concerned about frightening Sarah. She looked up and Florry noticed that she smiled in recognition. *Thank goodness. Maybe she won't make a scene this time.*

"Good morning," he said cheerily.

"My name is Sarah," she said, beaming like a child with a new toy.

"It's nice to see you looking so good, Sarah."

"Yes. It's going to snow."

"Not for a while, I hope. It's fairly warm outside." Turning toward Florry, he asked, "How are you today?"

"I'm good." She wanted to add that she wished she weren't good, but knew the Pastor would begin lecturing her.

He pulled up a chair and sat between the beds. "I wondered if you'd like to hear part of our lesson in adult Sunday school class. We had an interesting discussion and I'd like to share it with you."

"Fine," said Florry wearily. "I ain't been to Sunday school for a long time."

"We started out with this question. 'What's the meaning of life?' You'd be surprised at the answers I got." He looked at Florry keenly. "How would you answer?"

Florry was dumbfounded. *What kind of a question is that? How am I supposed to know?* She knew Pastor was waiting for an answer so she said the first thing that came into her head. "Life is being with your family, enjoying the world around you."

"Very good! That's an excellent definition. After I went around the room getting everyone's answers I told them a little story written by Anatole France. I won't read it now, but the main point is this: There was a king who wished to know the lessons of history and appointed a committee to find answers for him. Can you imagine what the committee determined?"

Florry, intrigued in spite of herself quickly said, "No," and noticed that Sarah had a troubled look on her face when she shook her head.

"They said to the king, 'Men are born, they suffer, they die and that is all.'" He looked at each woman in turn. "Isn't that sad? That committee never understood God's purpose for us."

"Does he really have a purpose for us?" Florry asked, unable to believe that she could ever know the mind of God.

The Pastor pulled a small book from his pocket and removed the marker. "St. Paul says it best in his letter to the Ephesians, Ch. I: 9, 10. 'He has made known to us his hidden purpose—such was his will and pleasure determined beforehand in Christ—to be put into effect when the time was ripe: namely, that the universe, all heaven and on earth, might be brought into a unity in Christ.' Do you understand? He is saying that uniting with Christ is the purpose of Creation."

Florry heard the words and in her own mind believed the words from Scripture. *But who's to say I can't unite with Christ when I want to?* She dare not bring her thoughts to the surface and made an effort to seem interested in what she was told. "I understand what you're telling us," she said. "I wish I could still read my Bible."

"We could get the Living Bible on tape for you, if you'd like," he offered.

Florry looked down at her hands, ashamed to say that Lucy had already brought her a tape recorder that she never tried to use. "That would be nice," she said graciously. "Thank you."

"As a matter of fact," he said as though he just thought of it, "I understand that you have a special day coming up next week."

Florry couldn't help being pleased at his remark. "Yep. Goin' to be ninety-six on March 15th. Jimmy's coming, too."

"How about I bring the Bible on tape for a present? I assume I'll be invited to the party?" he said with sly smile.

"That would be nice," she said until she remembered what that day meant. Her face must have shown her uncertainty because the Pastor gave her a questioning look. "Would you rather I didn't come?" he asked.

"No. It's okay," she said quickly. "I want you to come."

"Well then, I think you've seen enough of me for today." He rose and shook hands with Sarah. "It was nice seeing you again."

"Thy Will Be Done," she said piously.

"Yes, of course. You have the right idea." He took Florry's hands in his huge grasp and said, "Think about God's purpose for us. Will you?"

"Yes."

CHAPTER 29

Florry's situation was now desperate. *I said I didn't want to be ninety-six and now I can't help myself. If only Ben were here. He'd know what to do.*

On Wednesday, Lucy came to see her after work.

"You mean to tell me you left the office and drove thirty miles just to see me?" she began, secretly enjoying the attention.

"You're worth it Mom. Even a thirty mile drive," she said winking at her. "I came to tell you what we're planning for your birthday."

At the word 'birthday,' Sarah sat up straighter and seemed to pay more attention to her cards. She would lay a card down, pick it up again and re-align it with the others before repeating the routine. Lucy raised an eyebrow at her compulsive behavior and was about to say something when Florry gestured and mouthed the word 'birthday.' "She don't believe in 'em," she whispered.

Lucy nodded and watched the Solitaire game for a moment. When she was satisfied that the game continued without interruption, she went on. "Jimmy and Betsy got a Friday flight that arrives at O'Hare at seven in the evening. Jerry Ann is flying in from Minneapolis and will meet them at the airport."

"Good," she said, trying to sound excited. "I haven't seen Jerry Ann in ages. She wasn't able come with her mom and dad the last time they came to Wisconsin."

"If their flight's on time, they plan to rent a car and drive to Carson City—it's about a two hour drive. And if the plane's late they'll stay overnight and drive up on Saturday morning. How does that sound?"

"Did you tell me they would leave on Sunday?"

"Jimmy has to get back to work. So we'll have your birthday party on Sunday instead of Monday. I guess we can celebrate a day early."

"No birthday," Sarah said solemnly, looking up from the table.

"It's okay," Lucy assured her. "It's not your birthday, it's Florry's."

"I see," she said and went back to the cards.

"Pastor Sorensen was here Monday," Florry said. "He wants to come to the party."

"Sure. Why not?" She sat down on the edge of the bed. "Here's what I've planned so far. We'll go out to lunch on Sunday—the five of us—and then have cake and ice-cream here at the facility. I've talked to the dining room staff and they will serve any of the residents who care to join us."

"Will you call Pastor?"

"I certainly will. I think this will be fun for all of us and especially for you, the bir—excuse me, the party girl."

"You don't need to go to so much trouble."

"When I'm ninety-six, I'll definitely want people to help me celebrate."

"Tell me that when you get there," she said sadly. "You don't know what it's like."

Lucy took her hands. "Tell me what it's like. I want to know."

Florry intended to ignore the question, but before she knew it she was venting all her frustrations and worries. She began slowly. "It's like there's nothin' left. I can't do nothin' go no where, take care of myself —" She stifled a sob. "You won't know till you get to be an old lady yourself."

Lucy looked at her mother and Florry knew that she finally understood the utter despair she was experiencing. "I'm so sorry, Mom. I knew you were depressed but I always thought that since you weren't in pain and still fairly comfortable that you were just having a temporary bout of the blues."

"Nobody understands."

"I do. Is there anything I can do that will help?"

"No." *You can show me how to end this, but you won't.* She was afraid to say more. "When did you say Jimmy was coming?"

"Friday evening or Saturday morning."

"Good."

CHAPTER 30

"Hello Lucy?"

"Yes? Is that you Jimmy?"

"Yep, it's me. Our plane just got in. An hour an a half late—not bad for a Friday night, I guess."

"So you're going to stay over?" Before he could answer she hurried on. "Listen, Jimmy, there's a real bad storm on its way. Actually it started to snow at seven."

"Yeah, I know. They gave us the weather forecast on the plane. Not to worry. I rented a 4 x 4 and besides, I'm a mid-westerner from way back. A little snow won't stand in my way."

"Just listen to me for a minute," she insisted. "This storm's going to be bad. Warm air from the Gulf is coming up and will meet some Arctic air from Canada. It's a brutal combination—you know, 'The Perfect Storm'?"

"You're talking to a skier who used to live on the slopes at Winter Park until my knees gave out. Snow does not worry me in the least."

Lucy took the hand held phone and carried it to the window. What she saw was scary. "I'm looking out the window as I talk to you. I can't even see the patio from my kitchen window and the wind is picking up. Seriously, Jim they are predicting the spring snow storm of the century."

Jimmy laughed. "You are the worry wart. What I started to tell you was that since it's late, we'll be leaving first thing in the morning."

"How about Jerry Ann? Did she get in?"

"Yep, sure did. We're all looking forward to seeing you and Mom."

"Me, too. Everything's all set for her birthday. We'll go out to lunch on Sunday and then have a party in the facility. Cake and ice-cream—that sort of thing."

Lucy sensed that he wanted to say more and after a moment he said, "How is Mom?"

"She's really down. I don't seem to be able to get her un-de-pressed—if there is such a word. Maybe seeing you and Betsy and Jerry Ann will help."

"I hope so. Sorry this has all fallen on your shoulders. I wish I could do more."

"I don't do that much. Go to see her and all, but the care-givers at the facility are so good, that I rarely feel guilty."

"Guilty? You should get a 'good daughter medal'."

"Not really." She was embarrassed by his praise and said, "Call my cell when you leave O'Hare in the morning so that I'll know what time to expect you?"

"Sure thing." He stopped and then said, "Don't worry about anything. It'll all work out. Trust me."

Lucy chuckled. "Never trust anyone who says that. Anyway, goodnight Jimmy. See you tomorrow."

When she hung up the phone she went to the window again. The snow was coming down heavily with a fierce wind driving it into drifts. Lucy shuddered. *Hope the power doesn't go off.*

CHAPTER 31

At about the same time that Jimmy was talking to Lucy, Sarah began pacing the floor. Every time she came to the window, she peeked out and shivered. "Oooh, it's snowing."

"Well it ain't goin' to stop just cause you keep lookin' at it," Florry said crossly.

"I see," she replied and went back to her measured steps—seven forward, seven back.

"You're going wear out the tiles," Florry said wearily. "Quit!"

Sarah nodded and sank down into her easy chair facing the window. She repeated barely discernible words, but Florry reckoned they had something to do with the snow, which made her exasperated at her roommate's anxiety "You saw it snow before and nothin' happened. Why are you so nervous?"

Sarah pulled a corner of the drape to one side and pointed to the mounds of snow under their window. "Look! Snow," she said and repeated, "Snow!"

Florry rose from the bed and reached for her walker. As she slowly made her way to the window, Sarah tugged at the drapery cord exposing the wintry commons area. Florry surveyed the scene in amazement and exclaimed, "Holy Toledo! That ain't a snow storm, that's a blizzard!"

Both women watched in wonder as the howling wind whirled huge flakes of snow into eddy-like patterns. Sarah began shaking, so Florry held out her hand until Sarah grasped and clung to it like a frightened child. "It'll be okay, Sarah," Florry said calmly. "We'll be safe here."

At that moment, the lights flickered and went out. Sarah screamed in terror and pulled her hand away. She jumped up and inched cautiously toward her bed; where she quickly got under the covers like a wounded animal seeking a hiding place.

A few seconds later the lights came back followed by the appearance of an aide who explained that the storm had downed power lines and that the facility was now on generator power. "We'll be fine, ladies. There's nothing to worry about."

"See, Sarah? Everything's okay."

But Sarah continued to huddle under the covers and pulled a scarf over her head.

Florry patted her roommate and said, "I'm going to lie down, too. Go to sleep—I'll be here." She went to her own bed, clasped her panda and got comfortable. Snow storms no longer worried her. Once, she might have been frightened for her children if she thought they might get snowed in for any length of time. Now, she found nothing to fear from storms. *It's just snow and sooner or later it'll stop.*

She was waiting anxiously for Ben to come home. Every time she drew the curtain aside she became more frightened. The road leading to their home was almost buried under huge masses of snow and there seemed to be no end to the intensity of the storm. She glanced at the children watching TV and was thankful that the school sent them home early.

Ben called her before he left work and said, "Leaving now, Flor. It's wicked out there. Be home as soon as I can."

Florry looked at the kitchen clock. It was five-thirty; Ben had called at four. *He's been on the road for an hour and a half and it's only ten miles.* That thought was enough to further increase her fears. Then Lucy, looked up from the TV and said, "Where's Daddy?"

Trying to control her apprehension, she made her voice sound calm and believable. "He'll be home soon. Probably having trouble getting through the snow."

Lucy went to the window. "Wow! Maybe we won't have school tomorrow. What d'ya think Mom?"

"Probably not."

"When's supper?" Jimmy asked. "I'm starving. Don't we always eat at five-thirty?"

"We eat when Dad gets home," she reminded. "He should be here soon."

Fifteen minutes later she looked out again and thought she saw headlights. But the lights were stationary. She watched for a couple of minutes and when the vehicle did not move, she wondered if it was Ben and if he might be stuck. "I'm going out to the roadway," she said to the children. "I think I see Dad's car."

The children barely nodded as she put on boots and parka and headed out the door. She carried a flashlight but the wind whipped the snow around her and blocked out most of the light. *Sure looks like Ben's car, but it's hard to tell from here.* She trudged toward the headlights, one hand deep into her pocket, the other holding the practically useless flashlight. The snow stung her face like little sharp ice needles even though she kept her head turned away. After walking for several minutes she realized that she was getting no closer to the stopped vehicle, but getting bogged down in deeper and deeper drifts. *Something's wrong. I can't get to him.*

Totally panicked, she began yelling. "Ben, Ben, is that you? I can't see anything in this blizzard."

She went on calling and calling and received no answer. Finally giving way to total hysteria, she screamed, "Help, help me find Ben. Somebody help."

An aide was at her bedside and took both her hands. "There, there Florry," she whispered gently. "It's okay. I'm here now."

The snow and the wind and the vision of Ben's car were still before her. "No, you don't understand. It's Ben and he's out there. I must go to him." She jerked her hands away and started to get up. "I've got to go, you don't —"

The aide pressed the 'call' button and continued her soft pleading. "Just relax, Florry. Open your eyes."

In some part of her being she knew that if she opened her eyes that Ben and the snow would vanish and she would see her dream come to an end. But the images were so strong that she clung to the belief that Ben was coming for her. *He said that he'd come back. I don't want to wake up.*

The night nurse said, "Florry can you hear me?"

"Yes."

"You were having a nightmare. Are you frightened of the storm?"

"No." She opened her eyes and saw the nurse and the aide smiling at her. "What time is it?"

"Five minutes past three."

"In the afternoon?"

The aide laughed. "No, 'fraid not. It's the wee small hours of the morning."

"I guess I thought it was still—oh, I must have been dreaming."

The nurse nodded. "We want to make you more comfortable so we're going to give you a sedative. Okay?"

"Will I sleep?"

"The pill will make you very sleepy," she assured.

I can go back there. Ben's going to take me with him. I know it. "Okay," she said dutifully, trying not to give away her thoughts.

After she swallowed the medication, the nurse left and the aide tucked the covers around her. Then she went over to Sarah's bed and saw that she was curled up under the covers with only her nose and mouth visible.

Sarah looked at her, wide-eyed and fearful. "Florry?"

"Florry's fine. She just had a bad dream."

"Snowing?"

"It's still snowing, but we're all warm and cozy, so we're not going to worry about it. Okay."

Sarah smiled. "They Will Be Done."

The nurse pulled the curtain around, dividing the two beds. "Good night Ladies," she said and left the room.

Florry was glad to see her leave and knew this was the opportunity that she so desperately wanted. *Ben's out there.* The thought filled her with joy and while she waited for him, she popped an almond in her mouth. *I'm here, Ben, waiting for you.*

She was longing for sleep to come and closed her eyes in anticipation. Before she drifted off, Sarah came to her bedside and carefully laid her soft wooly scarf around Florry's neck. "It's snowing," she said simply.

Florry sighed. *That woman! She'll be the death of me.*

CHAPTER 32

Drifting between sleep and wakefulness, Lucy finally realized that she was cold and that searching for a warm spot was keeping her awake. She fumbled for the dial on the electric blanket and wondered why it wasn't heating. *Of course, the power's out.* Groaning inwardly, she grabbed the woolen quilt at the foot of the bed and brought it up over the electric blanket. The clock beside her bed was blinking three thirty-four. *That's when the lights went out.* She reached for the flashlight kept on the bedside table and shone it on her watch. *Four-thirty.* She decided that since it was Saturday, there was no point in getting up to a freezing house. *I'll stay where it's warm and pray for the power to come back. At least I have a gas range.*

A few minutes later, the phone rang. The sound startled her and before she even reached for it, she *knew.*

"Miss Hendricks?"

"Yes." The voice was not familiar, but it had an authoritative sound. A feeling of utter despair traveled through her body leaving her defenseless and drained. *She finally did it. Mom figured out a way.*

"This is Carolyn Jahnke from the Carson County Care Facility. Are you alone?"

"Yes, I live here alone." The voice coughed slightly and continued in a subdued tone. "I have some bad news about your mother."

"She's dead, isn't she?"

There was a brief pause before the caller continued. "I'm very sorry to say so. We found her a short time ago. She appears to have suffocated."

"What? Suffocated? How can that be?"

"We're waiting for the doctor who's on his way. He'll be able to give us more answers."

"Why do you think she suffocated?" Lucy could not imagine

dying by suffocation and found it impossible to believe that her mother could have died from lack of oxygen.

"There was a scarf around —"

The phone made a crackling sound and went dead. "What did you say?" Lucy asked frantically.

She tried to get a dial tone without success. *I'll try my cell phone.* She jumped out of bed and went to the living room and retrieved the cell from her handbag. She hastily dialed the facility but got no answer. *Oh my God! Mom's dead? And she suffocated?*

She sat down on the sofa, laid her head back and closed her eyes. Her breath came in involuntary gasps as the full impact of the terrible news filled her being, making her weak and unsteady. She wondered if she was dreaming until she realized that her feet were bare and the floors were freezing. While she sat in the cold house, feeling totally alone and abandoned, she remembered the last time she spoke to her mother and what they talked about. That was when she expressed the hopelessness that had become her life. Her mother's state of mind combined with the last words of the phone call. 'There was a scarf around —' made Lucy cringe. *That can't be—it just can't be. I've got to go to her.*

When she went to the window and looked at the scene before her, she cringed. *I'll have to get the snow off the driveway before I can get to the street.* She hurriedly made some coffee in the old aluminum pot and while it was percolating, washed in cold water and dressed. Feeling more like an icicle than a person, she poured coffee and carried it to the back door where she pressed the garage door opener.

My word. There's a ton of snow. She wondered if she'd be able to remove enough snow to reach the street—even with the snow blower. *Got to try.* She took a few more sips of coffee, got her boots, heavy gloves and jacket from the closet and went out to start the snow machine. There was about twenty feet of drive to clear before she could reach the street that looked like it had been plowed at least once. As far as she could tell, the snow had stopped and there seemed to be very little wind. In fact when she took the time to look up, bright twinkling stars told her that the storm had passed.

She worked steadily, afraid that if she stopped she'd break down and cry. *I've got to be strong and get to the facility as soon as I can.* It took a half hour to blow away enough snow to back out. She returned to the house, drank her cold coffee and called Jimmy.

One ring. Two rings. "Hello?" said a sleep-fogged voice.

"Jimmy. Something terrible has happened. It's about Mom."

"Did she have an accident? What?"

"No. Worse than that. She's dead, Jimmy."

"It can't be. Are you sure?"

"They called me about four-thirty. The line went dead, but they think she suffocated."

"What? What kind of a place allows their patients to suffocate?"

"That's what I want to know. Anyway, I just got my driveway opened and I'm going over. Call me when you folks leave."

"I will. We'll get there as quickly as we can."

"Oh, Jimmy?"

"Yeah?"

"Better check on the roads before you leave."

"For sure."

As soon as she hung up the phone, she gathered her things and went to the car, hoping her snow tires would see her through the thirty mile drive. She put her car in reverse and gave it enough gas to successfully clear the drive. *So far so good.*

She followed Main Street, which was cleared of snow and felt confident about driving to Carson City. *Roads aren't bad at all.* On the outskirts of town, she drove toward the intersection where she would turn east. Even before she got close to the cross roads, she saw flashing red lights. *Oh no! Now what!*

The road was blocked by a wooden barrier and a sheriff's vehicle waved her down. When she opened the window a uniformed officer came and said, "Road's closed, Ma'am. Been several accidents so far and we can't let anyone pass."

After hearing about the road closing, she broke down and cried. The pent-up emotions successfully kept at bay exploded. "But you don't understand. It's my mother. I think she's dead. I have to go to her."

The officer looked at her kindly. "In Carson City?" She nodded numbly. "I'm sorry. You wouldn't be able to get through anyway. The drifting is over the top of your car in some places."

"What shall I do," she wailed. "I've got to go."

The officer considered for a moment and said, "Wait just a minute. Maybe there's something we can do."

She watched while he went to his car and talked on his mobile phone. When he came back, the look on his face encouraged her to hope. "If you wait a few minutes, the snow plow will be here. He's going to make a run to Carson City. You can follow him, if you're careful."

More tears came to her eyes as she sniffled and smiled at the same time. "Thank you. Thank you so much."

When the huge snow plow appeared the officer waved her on. "Be careful," he said. "Stay well back of him."

"I will."

She drove slowly which gave her time to fully think through the words, 'There was a scarf around —'

CHAPTER 33

Florry began to feel the effects of the sedative soon after the nurses left. She was relaxed and eager to get back to the dream where she *knew* Ben was waiting. *He said he'd be back—now we'll be together forever.* She smiled inwardly at the prospect of leaving behind the world of nurses and hospitals. The one regret she had concerned her children. But she did not allow herself to dwell on that thought.

The almond candy she slipped into her mouth was almost completely melted. She always like to 'suck the juice' out before biting down on the almond that would be soft and chewy.

She reviewed all the things she would tell Ben when she saw him. *First, I need to let him know how much I missed him these past ten years.* As the thoughts floated by she jerked awake and felt a drool of saliva in the corner of her mouth. *Got to finish this candy before I fall asleep.* She grabbed a tissue and wiped her mouth. *I'm worst than a kid.*

She drifted off again and almost immediately saw Ben. He was at the foot of her bed, wearing the generous smile that she so loved. "I came to take you fishing," he said. "Do you have clothes?"

"Sure. They's in the cupboard." She started to get out of bed, when she began choking. *The damn almond's stuck in my throat.* She clutched at her neck struggling to scream or call someone. "Ben, Ben," she tried to say, but heard nothing from herself. *Am I dying? I can't breathe.* She gestured frantically at Sarah, hoping to get her attention, but realized the curtain blocked her view. In a wheezing kind of breath, gasping for air that would not come, she called, "Someone, help me." Again, there was no sound.

Thoughts whirled around her, flashing moments of joy and moments of pain. She tried to grab at them as they flew by, always out of reach. *I need to remember my life; I don't want it taken from me. Now I'm going to choke to death, but I changed my mind. I don't want to die. God, where are you? This is not fair!*

She could still see Ben faintly—still at the foot of the bed. He made no move to help, nor did he seem aware of her struggle. "I came to take you fishing," he repeated.

But I don't want to go with you! I want to stay here. She no longer had the energy to call out or move her arms. The room became darker with blackness closing in to smother her. She couldn't breathe; she no longer cared. Nothing was important—there was only . . .

***

Sarah fell asleep soon after she gave her scarf to Florry to protect her from the snow. She was a light sleeper and thought she heard Florry coughing. She listened for a moment and decided that Florry was clearing her throat. *I should see if she's okay.*

As she was about to get up and go to Florry's bed, she remembered Visitor's words. "She doesn't want you to call."

She smiled broadly, knowing that her help was not needed. "Thy Will Be Done," she murmured and went back to sleep.

CHAPTER 34

Lucy followed the snow plow, annoyed at how slowly he traveled. When she checked the odometer, she was not surprised to see the dial read eighteen miles per hour. *At least I'm getting there. If it weren't for the plow I'd be back home.*

It was still dark and as she drove over the deserted road, she had the feeling that she was in a snow tunnel. Branches, laden with snow occasionally dropped additional piles of snow onto the highway. There was only one lane open, so all she had to do was keep the plow in her headlights.

She turned the phrase, 'There was a scarf,' over and over in her mind and kept coming to the same conclusion. *This is Sarah's doing. I just know it. If she wrapped her scarf around Mom's neck, that could have suffocated her.* As she considered that possibility, she wondered if someone could be suffocated that easily—even if the person was asleep. *Doesn't make sense, but how else could it have happened?*

Her cell played its silly little tune. "Hello?"

"Jimmy here. Where are you?"

"On the road to Carson City following a big snow plow."

"Really? Well, you're lucky. At least you're moving in the right direction."

"How about you? Have you left the airport?"

"Not yet. I-94 is not open, but I understand that by eight o'clock, they'll let us through. We're eating breakfast right now; hopefully we'll be able to leave in a half hour or so. How far are you from the facility?"

"The last sign said five miles. It's not light yet and I haven't been able to recognize any of the usual landmarks."

"How long have you been on the road?"

"Left home about five-thirty, now it's seven-thirty. But I'll be there soon."

"Sorry we can't do any better. If all goes well, we should get there around ten or eleven. I'm really anxious to talk to those people. The more I think about it the madder I get."

"Me, too." She sighed. "Let's don't talk about Mom. I'm trying to put everything on hold until I get there. Right now, I'm doing my best just to keep this car on the road and my courage intact."

"I understand. We'll see you ASAP. Take care."

Lucy put the phone in the caddy. Jimmy's anger at the facility rekindled her first reaction to the news of suffocation. *Somebody's going to have to do some tall explaining.*

CHAPTER 35

Sarah awakened and heard two women talking about Florry. The cloth screen enclosed Florry's bed, so she couldn't see anything. She listened carefully.

"When did you find her?" Sarah recognized the voice of Mrs. Jahnke, the head nurse.

"Just a few minutes ago," said the other voice. "I looked in to see if the sedative had taken effect and saw that she wasn't breathing. I listened with my stethoscope and tried to take her pulse. Nothing."

"Did you notice the red marks on her skin—like small hemorrhages."

"Yes. What causes them?"

"Sometimes you see them when a person suffocates."

"Is that what happened?"

Mrs. Jahnke said, "I'm not sure, but I called the doctor as soon as you reported. He said he'd come as soon as he could."

"Which may take a while under present conditions."

"Was that scarf around her neck?"

"Yes. Just as you see it. I was careful not to disturb anything. Do you think she may have suffocated?"

"Possibly. She would have been drowsy from the sedative and unable to offer much resistance."

No one spoke for a moment and Sarah wondered if they left. *Something's wrong with Florry.* She wanted to get up and pull back the curtain but was afraid the nurses would be angry.

Mrs. Jahnke said, "I'll call her daughter."

"What will you tell her?"

"I don't know. I just don't know." Sarah heard her footsteps as she left the room.

"Florry?" she whispered tentatively.

The aide pulled the curtain open slightly, slipped into Sarah's space and replaced the curtain. "Oh, you're awake. Did you want something?"

Sarah repeated. "Florry?"

"We've called the doctor. As soon as he comes, we'll know more about her."

There's something wrong. They don't want me to know. "Hospital?"

"We're not sure, but when the doctor comes —"

Her words of explanation were interrupted by men talking quietly as they came into the room. Sarah had a feeling of panic and tried not to look as the aide drew the curtain a few inches and gestured toward the bed. In spite of her fears, she involuntarily took a quick peek and saw two men dressed in white. She also noticed that a sheet was pulled up over Florry's face. Even with the curtain drawn she could hear Florry's bed being wheeled out of the room into the hallway. *Where are they taking her?*

***

Doctor Stevenson, snowed in like most everyone, did not get to the facility until seven a.m. He went directly to the room where Florry had been taken and examined the body. The aide and the head nurse, Mrs. Jahnke were at his side.

"You found her just like this?" he asked.

"Yes, Doctor," the aide replied. "This is exactly how she looked when I first saw her."

The doctor read the nurses' reports, noted the red marks on her face and neck and carefully pried open her mouth. "Aha," he said with a measure of satisfaction.

He reached for his forceps, extracted an object from Florry's trachea and held it up. "She choked on this," he said.

"What is it?" Mrs. Jahnke asked.

"Looks like a nut of some kind," he said dropping it into the tray.

"Jordan almond," said the aide. "She was always eating them."

The head nurse said, "Apparently no one heard her."

"Choking deaths are pretty silent," the doctor said. "Usually the victim will make wheezing noises or wave his hands, but they can't really make themselves heard."

"But her roommate was in the room. Wouldn't she know something was wrong?"

"Not necessarily. But didn't you tell me that this woman had been given a sedative?"

"Yes, Doctor. Shortly after three, she had a nightmare and was quite upset. We were trying to make her less anxious."

"With sedation, she may not have struggled too long before succumbing."

"I still wonder why no one heard her," the aide said thoughtfully. "How long would she be gasping for air?"

"It takes maybe four or five minutes to choke to death, but with the sedative, it probably took less time."

"If only we'd checked on her sooner," the aide said. "We might have prevented this."

"What time did you find her?" Doctor Stevenson asked.

"I reported that she wasn't breathing. That was at four-fifteen."

Mrs. Jahnke shook her head. "What a terrible thing to have happen."

"It was an accident," the doctor said. There's not much you could have done to prevent it, besides being in the room when she began choking."

"What do we tell her family?"

"Tell them the truth," the doctor said.

CHAPTER 36

Lucy brought her car to a stop in the facility parking lot after turning off the main road. She wished she could have thanked the snow plow driver, but he was headed directly toward town. She was amazed at the mountains of snow around the perimeter of the parking area. *Hope there aren't any cars buried under there.*

After the slow, torturous drive, she felt exhausted and frazzled. Her nervous state further fueled her blinding rage at Sarah—at the institution, at the snow storm that kept her prisoner in her car. *I've got to know what happened.*

She slipped in the front door and went directly to 103. Only one bed was in the room and Sarah was sitting on it playing Solitaire. Her calm, meticulous manner pushed Lucy over the edge of her long held restraint.

"What did you do to my mother?" she heard herself scream.

Sarah looked up, wide-eyed and smiling faintly. "Florry?"

"Yes. You know who I mean. What did you do?"

Sarah frowned and mumbled, "Doctor?"

Lucy lost control and near hysteria, shrieked, "I want to know right now. It was your scarf wasn't it? You did this. And now Mom's gone."

"Oh, I'm so sorry," she said like a little girl apologizing for something she did not do.

Lucy closed her eyes at the sight, knowing that she would hit Sarah if she continued looking at her. "I hate you. This is all your fault —"

Mrs. Jahnke came into the room and put an arm around Lucy's shoulders. "Come with me," she said gently. Lucy felt ashamed and finally subdued after her outburst and went quietly to her office.

"Please sit down. May I offer you coffee?"

"Yes. Please."

After pouring a cup and handing it to Lucy, she sat opposite her and waited before speaking. "There's been a terrible accident," she began.

"I know. When I got a call at four-thirty I was told 'there was a scarf around' and then the line went dead."

"That was right after we found her. Unfortunately we couldn't have given you more information even if the phones were working."

"I've been frantic to know what happened to Mom. Please tell me."

"I understand your frustration. This has been a horrendous night. Not only were the phones out, but we experienced a power outage and switched over to our generator system."

"I know how bad it was," Lucy said tiredly. "I followed a snow plow or I wouldn't even be here."

"The doctor finally arrived, quite some time after you were called. Actually he got here on his snow mobile."

Lucy leaned forward. "What did he say?"

"That's why I brought you back here. I wanted to explain everything from the beginning."

Lucy swallowed and steeled herself for what she believed would be an unpardonable   revelation. *This facility must be accountable for what they let happen.* After a few sips of coffee, she felt more in control. "I'm listening."

"Your mother had a bad dream; actually it was more like a nightmare. This was about three o'clock this morning. We gave her a sedative so that she could get back to sleep. Apparently all the commotion awakened Sarah. Knowing the way she mothers Florry, she probably thought the scarf would protect her against the snow storm."

"I knew it!" Lucy exclaimed, feeling the anger rebuilding. "It was all Sarah's fault. With the sedative, my poor mother was either too tired or too disoriented to loosen the scarf." She heard all she needed to hear, collected her coat and handbag and got up to leave.

"Please sit down, Lucy," Mrs. Jahnke begged. "Let me finish."

"What's there to finish? That woman murdered my mother." She was glaring at Mrs. Jahnke and knew she was losing control.

"Please sit down," she repeated. "I know this is hard, but there is an explanation."

"It better be good," she fumed. She sat on the edge of the chair and waited.

Mrs. Jahnke, voice calm and soothing, continued. "What we believe happened next was that your mother took one of her almond candies and kept it in her mouth, dozed off and began choking. Sarah must not have heard her."

"Why not?" Lucy shot back, "she was in the same room."

"Please, try to understand. The doctor told us that a choking person is not able to make much noise. Sarah may have been asleep or may have assumed your mother was merely trying to clear her throat."

"But she was in the same room," Lucy insisted, not willing to be convinced.

"In the same room divided by a curtain," Mrs. Jahnke said looking at her intently. "Sarah could not see her."

"What did the Doctor say?" she asked hoping to hear a more acceptable account of what actually occurred. "He extracted a whole almond from her trachea." She said the words quietly and added, "I'm sorry."

Lucy bowed her head and wept.

CHAPTER 37

Sarah watched as Mrs. Jahnke led Lucy from her room. Lucy was angry with her and she was afraid that it had something to do with Florry. *They took her away.* She recalled the time that Florry fell and was taken to the hospital and wondered if she went there again. She continued to play cards while she tried to think where Florry might be.

Just then two men wheeled in a bed—nicely made, but not Florry's bed. She wanted to hide, but her curiosity held her captive. "Where is she?" she asked timidly.

One of the men turned and said, "Mrs. Jahnke is coming to talk to you."

"I see." As soon as the men left she dealt three more cards and went on with the game. When she looked up she saw the head nurse. She carried a red rose that she carefully placed on the bed.

"Good Morning Sarah," she said pleasantly.

"Where's Florry?"

"Florry won't be coming back," she said.

"Hospital?"

"No. Florry died last night. We put a rose on the beds of patients who die so that we can remember them."

"Died?" She tried to think of that word and did not immediately understand. She smiled and pretended she knew how to answer. "I'm so sorry."

"I know you are. Florry was a good friend and we'll all miss her."

"Ooookay." She reconsidered a moment. "Florry's gone?"

"Yes."

"Hospital?"

"No. She won't be coming back here." Sarah thought the nurse was lying to her and went back to her cards. *She's trying to scare me.*

Mrs. Jahnke watched her for a few moments and then said, "I'll be in my office, Sarah. Please come and see me whenever you want to talk."

Sarah nodded and the nurse left.

***

Before leaving for the day, Mrs. Jahnke talked to the nurse on duty. "I don't think that Sarah quite understands Florry's death. The word 'died' did not seem to register. She probably believes that Florry has gone somewhere but in any case, I doubt that will be upsetting to her. Women like Sarah have short term memories."

The nurse asked, "Will she get a new roommate?"

"I'm sure. We have a waiting list, so we'll try and find someone compatible."

"Sarah is so docile and sweet, that should be no problem."

***

After Mrs. Jahnke left her room, Sarah collected all the cards, even though she hadn't finished the game. The word 'died' kept repeating itself until she felt mesmerized by the thought. *Died, died, died, Florry died.* And then she remembered. *Jonathan died too. And Joey and my mother and father. I didn't die, but I wanted to.*

When Sarah was fifty-five, her life changed drastically. She was still working at the library that she considered her refuge from a drab, mundane life. She still wrote poems but was careful to keep them hidden from Jonathan. All her poetry went into a safety deposit box and she hid the key in her purse.

She was still an attractive woman. Her black curly hair had few gray strands and when she engaged in conversation, her dark eyes sparkled with vitality and charm. At the library, she was sought after as an understanding and intelligent advisor on books and library matters. She managed to keep a trim figure and always dressed as neatly as her limited wardrobe would allow. Jonathan acted more like a roommate imposing on her only once a week for what he considered his obligatory rights as a husband

The library closed at nine; Sarah lived only two blocks away and she often was the last to leave. One snowy night in January, the library director called.

"Sarah? This is Janice. I just heard a weather report and they're expecting about ten inches of snow. It's snowing hard right now, if you haven't noticed."

Sarah glanced out the window and saw the wind driven snow begin to pile up on the outside walls. "I see what you mean."

It's eight-fifteen and I think you should turn out the lights and go home. You still have a couple of blocks to walk."

"Okay. Whatever you think. But I won't have any trouble getting home—not yet anyway."

"Why don't you call your husband and ask him to come for you?"

"I will if necessary. Don't worry."

"I won't. Close up shop and if we're not snowed in, I'll see you tomorrow."

"Good night." *Jonathan pick me up? I'd rather die than call him. I love walking in the snow when it's clean and fresh. Besides, I've got my boots and scarf and storm coat.*

She walked around the main floor reading room and saw that it was virtually empty. Two students sitting side by side at a table looked like they were having a clandestine date and not working on a paper that Sarah helped them research. *Kids!* The only other person was a man slouched in a chair who appeared to be asleep. She always approached strangers warily, never sure what to expect. This man was no exception and as she got closer saw that he was dressed like a vagrant—shabby and dirty. She was ready to hold her breath if he stank. "Sir? The library is closing now. You'll have to leave."

He did smell and when he looked up at her bleary eyed and when he understood that she was serious, he became belligerent. "Ain't this public property? I can stay here if I want to."

"You don't understand. We're expecting a snow storm so we're closing early," she said as reasonably as possible.

He rose unsteadily and when he stood, Sarah saw that he was a much bigger man than he appeared to be when seated. He eyed her up and down and when she raised her chin and prepared to repeat her statement, he said, "All right. I'm leaving. But I'll be back tomorrow."

"Fine. We'll expect you," she said graciously and turned her head away.

The students traipsed out the front door, after stuffing notes and books into their backpacks. The man who she thought might be a homeless person followed close behind. *Hope he has a place for the night.* She locked the front door behind them and went through the list of closing procedures—checking bathrooms, offices, and storage areas.

After all the lights were out and the heat turned down, she went down the stairs so that she could leave by the back entrance. The stairwell and the hall were almost dark. An outside light, shining through a window cast enough light for her to find her keys and reach for the door knob. Before she could open the door, the man who had left by the front door, stepped out from the corner shadows.

"Where did you come from?" she managed to say, before he grabbed her with one arm, the other hand holding a knife.

He looked into her face and she had to fight to keep her revulsion in check. "Been waitin' for ya," he mumbled.

In rapid succession, various thoughts came to mind. *Shall I struggle? Try to reason with him? Act submissive?*

She needn't have worried about what she should do because he wrenched her to the floor and still holding the knife above her face, pinned her down with his knee driving into her stomach. His dirt-caked face lined with filthy, greasy hair loomed over her until she had to close her eyes. The stench of squalor emanating from his body so repulsed her that she felt ill. She knew what he was going to do; she closed her eyes and willed herself into submission.

He removed his knee making it easier to breathe. *Is he going to let me go?* She inched forward a little and started to get up when he punched her in the face. "I got a knife. I can cut you up and hurt you real bad. Don't move!"

She lay very still, reeling from the blow and was conscious of a warm trickle coming from her nose. The urge to reach up and touch her face intensified and it was only with supreme restraint that she resisted the impulse. *If I keep my eyes closed and don't breathe I can pretend this is not happening; I'll be safe. I won't look at him; I won't smell him.* She held her breath as long as she could and when she had to breathe, did so in small gasps, but his nauseous odor still permeated her nose and body.

What was he doing now? She heard the slipping sound of a belt being unfastened and then the faint whir of a zipper. *Why is this happening so slowly? I want it to be over.* She felt trapped in a drama that moved in slow motion. *Of course, this is a dream—soon I'll awaken.* Suddenly, the time warp exploded into frenzied action. The man must have dropped the knife because now he was tearing at her slacks, ripping them off her body with savage force. She closed off her mind. *I won't feel this; I won't ever allow myself to remember. He can do what he wants.*

Her resolve was short lived as the weight of him pressed down into her until she felt she would break in two pieces. His smell was overpowering reminding her of dark and dirty sewers, filth and excrement. Choking on the foulness coming from him she tried to scream and found that no sound came from her mouth. He repeated over and over, "I'm doin' this because you're a fuckin' bitch. Don't move or I'll —"

The scene changed to slow motion once again and now she thought he would hammer at her long enough to kill her. The pain got worse with each thrust and she knew she would die. Her last thought was praying for death to come quickly.

❄❄❄

She felt stings of icy cold snow on her face before she remembered where she was. The back library door was open and occasionally the wind deposited little heaps of snow into the hallway where she lay. "I have to go home," she mumbled to herself. "Jonathan will be worried." She sat up slowly, conscious of a terrible throbbing in her head. *I can hardly see.* When she gingerly touched her face, she winced in pain as her fingers explored a swollen eye. There was a light switch near the door. She pulled herself up using the door knob and shuddered at the pain that seemed to encompass her whole body. *What happened to me?*

As soon as she flipped the light switch, she looked down at her clothing and gasped. Her slacks were torn and soiled and as she slipped them off and stuffed them into a trash basket, waves of nausea forced her to vomit over the discarded clothing.

She wanted to escape out into the night and leave the scene that caused her—*what did it cause? No, I have to clean up this mess before I go home.* She went to the janitor's closet and got some rags that she wet in the sink. The floor in the hall looked dirty—smears of mud and blood and scraps of clothing. She got down on her hands and knees, working past the pain that lingered, wiped up the mess and threw the rags in the trash container. *Libraries should be clean and neat.* She smoothed her storm coat down over her bare legs and wrapped a scarf around her neck, cushioning her bruised face. The key was on the floor; she picked it up, locked the door and headed home.

She stepped onto the snow covered sidewalk, feeling free and untouchable. *Snow, the snow will cleanse me. I'll be whole again.* The memory of that wintry walk was etched into her consciousness, forever obscuring the horror of what came before. She remembered the wind spinning the falling flakes into little eddies that felt purifying as they whirled around her. She looked up into the sky hungering for the icy tingles that would both sooth her puffy face and cool her burning forehead. The fantasy of that night shimmered in her mind like a crystal—intense and mysterious; she hoped she'd never reach her home.

She smiled as she walked through the deserted streets and finally stopped at her front door where she collapsed. Jonathan found her there.

CHAPTER 38

"Lucy?" An aide came and sat beside her and put an arm around her shoulders. "I'm terribly sorry. We all loved your mother and we'll miss her."

Lucy nodded, still too overcome to reply.

"I came to take you to your mother's room. You can spend as much time there as you wish."

Lucy went with her to another part of the building. Before she went in she said, "I'm expecting my brother. Would you send him here when he arrives?"

"Of course. May I get you anything? Coffee?"

"No, I'm fine. Thanks."

She had been dreading seeing her mother—now that she knew the whole story. *It's all so bizarre. I can't believe it really happened.*

She opened the door and went into the room knowing she would again break down. Her mother lay on the bed and except for the tiny red marks on her face, appeared quite normal. *She could be sleeping.* Lucy sank into the bedside chair and rested her head on the sheet. The thoughts that crowded her mind were at the same time muddled and starkly clear. She tried to make sense of the accident while at the same time tried to understand that her mother had succeeded in her wish.

She felt an overwhelming need to talk to her and began softly, "Mom, I don't know what to say. I can't come to terms with the fact that you will no longer be here. That I won't be coming over to see you anymore. You can't know how empty and alone that makes me feel. I was so focused on you and my visits that I can't imagine how I will fill that ache in my heart." The tears were beginning again and she hastily went on, believing that her mother was listening. "I know you were tired of living and I hope that wherever you are, you've found a better life—maybe with Dad—who knows? I only want what you thought you wanted. I can only say that I hope you rest in peace."

She gave way to sobbing and thought she'd never have enough tears to overcome her grief when she felt a hand on her shoulder. Jimmy had come. He took her in his arms and they cried together.

"She looks like she's napping," Jimmy said through his tears. "Doesn't seem to have a care in the world."

"I know. It's all so crazy."

Betsy and Jerry Ann came into the room. Betsy was the first to speak. "Sorry we had to meet under these conditions, Lucy. I thought it was going to be a wonderful reunion."

"So did I," Lucy said, trying hard to gain control. "But it's good to have all of you here. I'm glad you came."

"So are we." She looked at them standing with arms around each other and smiled. "I always forget how much you two resemble each other. If Jimmy had longer hair, I bet you could pass for identical twins."

Lucy laughed and felt some of her tension lightened. "I think Mom was glad that we weren't the same sex. At least that was one way she could tell us apart."

"Lucy and I used to fool her. We'd wear hats or something on our heads and pretend we were the other twin."

"What a couple of rascals you must have been. Ganging up on the poor woman," Betsy said. "Twins are hard enough without those aggravations."

Lucy grew thoughtful. "Jimmy? You and I should write some of our memories of Mom. Sort of a journal."

"Good idea. Mom was one of a kind."

"Those are the kind of thoughts that will carry you through this," Betsy said. "Think about the good times."

Lucy noticed a man standing in the doorway. "The undertaker is here to take —" She cleared her throat. "Let's go into the next room."

Jimmy guided her away from her mother's bed. "We've said our goodbyes. There's nothing more we can do for her. I want to hear about this suffocation business."

They all sat in the lounge, Jimmy and his family waiting for her to speak. She gave them Mrs. Jahnke's explanation of how the accident occurred. "It's really ironic. I think she wanted to die, but to have it happen with candy I brought her is too much —" That thought brought on a fresh wave of tears. Jimmy too, was overcome.

Betsy said, "You'll have to stop blaming yourself," she said. "I know that's hard advice, but the only way you could have stopped her was by being there at that moment in time."

"I know," Lucy said, still sobbing. "But it's all so stupid."

"Didn't you tell Jimmy that she was depressed and thinking of ways to commit suicide?"

"Yes. But —"

"You and Jimmy have to believe that she is with God, that she is reunited with Ben and that she received her wish to die. That will have to sustain you."

Lucy nodded and Jimmy took both her hands and said, "We'll face this together, Sis. We'll help each other remember Mom the way she'd want us to. Okay?"

"Okay."

There was a knock on the door and when Lucy said, "Come in," a young aide appeared.

"I don't want to intrude," she began, "but we wondered if you wanted us to pack up your mother's things for you."

Lucy sighed. "Please. That would be nice."

The aide hesitated for a moment before asking, "What should be done with the stuffed animals?"

"I'll go to the room with you. I have to talk to Sarah anyway."

***

Sarah looked up when Lucy and the aide came into the room, followed by Jimmy and his family. She was reading the Watchtower and as soon as she saw Jimmy, she put the book in the drawer and walked toward the bathroom.

Lucy said, "Jimmy, why don't you wait in the hall? Sarah gets nervous around strange men."

"Okay. I'll be in the lobby."

Sarah looked visibly relieved and said "Lucy?"

"Yes. I'm Lucy and this is my sister-in-law, Betsy and my niece, Jerry Ann."

Sarah favored them with one of her most winning smiles and said, "I see."

"I'm sorry if I was cross with you," Lucy began. "I was so upset about Mom I'm afraid I made a dreadful commotion."

"Nooo," Sarah said. She pointed to the bed that contained the red rose. "Florry?"

"She won't be coming back," Lucy said carefully. "Mom died."

Sarah smiled again as though she was hearing good news. "I'm so sorry."

"I'm going to send Mom's stuffed animals to the children's wing of the hospital," she said to Sarah. "This girl is going to pack them up."

Sarah watched while the aide opened several large plastic bags and began filling them with stuffed animals. "No! No!" She jumped up and stood between the aide and the animals. "Florry's, Florry's," she said becoming more and more agitated.

Lucy began to realize the depth of Sarah's caring for her room-mate. *She doesn't understand that Mom is gone.* Lucy took the white panda from the shelf. *This was Mom's favorite—always had it with her.* "I want you to keep this bear for Florry," Lucy said. "You take good care of it."

"Oookay," she said and carried the bear to her own bed. There she carefully laid it on the pillow and pulled up a blanket to cover it. She appeared to be content and did not interfere with packing the remainder of Florry's belongings.

Lucy was exhausted. "Let's get out of here. I need some fresh air."

CHAPTER 39

In the early afternoon, the four of them met with the funeral director and the Pastor and made plans for the funeral. The church service would be on Monday morning followed by a luncheon at the church. Florry wanted to be buried next to Ben in the Carson City cemetery and Lucy thought she'd want a gravesite ceremony. When they called the cemetery groundskeeper, he said the actual burial of the coffin would have to wait because the ground was still frozen solid. "You can reschedule the burial for later in the spring," he said. "We have a storage facility for that purpose."

"Well, so much for that idea," Lucy said.

"We'll plan to come back," Jimmy said.

"That would be nice." She shrugged. "I guess there's not much more we can do right now. Everything's pretty well planned." After thanking the Pastor and director, they drove both cars back to Lucy's. The roads had been cleared and with the March sun, a lot of the snow had begun to melt. When she drove up the driveway into the garage, she couldn't believe it was the same driveway that gave her so much trouble ten hours earlier. *This must be a dream. Soon I'll awaken and everything will be the same as it was yesterday.*

The rest of the day had an aura of unreality—as though time was standing still. She was tired, but knew she'd never be able to nap, so she busied herself with making sure her three house guests were comfortable. Every time she looked at the clock she thought it had stopped. *It's only four o'clock; I've lived a lifetime since this morning.*

Lucy was expecting Jimmy and his family, so she had extra provisions. When she began dinner preparations by putting a roast in the oven, Betsy came to help.

"Don't go to any trouble for us," she said.

"I'm not. What could be easier than pot roast and vegetables?'

"Nothing, I guess. But you must be exhausted."

"I am tired, but I don't think I could rest. I'm still keyed up thinking about —"

"I'm sure you must be. As soon as you get that roast in the oven, why don't we all sit in the living room and visit? Relax and unwind."

"Sounds good to me. I'll be there in a minute. How about a glass of wine?"

"Sure. I think Jimmy and Jerry Ann will want some, too. It's been a long day for all of us."

Lucy prepared a tray with cheese and crackers, glasses and a bottle of white wine and set it on the coffee table. "Help yourselves," she said as she sank down on the couch. "Oooh, heaven.! I may never want to move. If I get too bombed or fall asleep, somebody get our dinner out of the oven."

"I'll do it," Jimmy said. "I'll be in charge."

Betsy poured wine in glasses, handed them around and said, "That roommate of your mother's, Sarah I think her name is—what do you know about her?"

"Not a whole lot," Lucy replied. "She's a lot younger than Mom—only eighty. And she's a Jehovah's Witness."

"Really!" Betsy exclaimed. "But of course. I saw her reading Watchtower." She frowned and looked a bit embarrassed when she asked, "Is she senile?"

"I'm not sure what her problem is—not exactly. Sometimes she seems to know what you're talking about and other times she's in the 'twilight zone'."

"Does she have family?"

"I don't think she has any living relatives, but once I heard the aides' gossiping and eavesdropped. They said that she's been a resident for quite some time and that she was cared for by her husband until he died. He apparently entrusted her with a book, actually a small notebook that she keeps in her bedside drawer."

"Have you seen it?"

"I've gotten a glimpse when she puts her cards away, but she never takes it out or reads it."

"Sounds like a strange lady to me," Jimmy said.

"I'm sure that we'd know more about her, if we could read the book. But as far as I know, it's never left the drawer."

"Poor woman," Betsy said sympathetically. "I wonder if she's aware that she's alone in the world?"

"Probably not. She must have some sort of income and guardian because she gets new clothes from time to time and she doesn't seem to want for anything."

"But no one visits her?" Betsy asked.

"I don't think so."

Jimmy said, "She's afraid of men?"

"Yes, she is." Lucy shook her head and pursed her lips. "That and some other things she does really bug me."

"Like what?" Betsy asked.

"She's got this thing about snow. Wears boots and a scarf whenever it's snowing—even though she's inside."

Jerry Ann, who had been sitting quietly listening to the conversation said, "Why would she do that?"

"I don't know. You probably noticed that she gives unrelated answers to questions?" Betsy nodded. "In addition, she's compulsive about keeping things neat and straightened up."

"That is strange. Do the nurses say anything about her?"

"No. They won't discuss patients' problems, so all I know is what I've observed."

"I can't help but feel that she really cared for Florry," Betsy said. "Did you see the way she reacted when the aide wanted to pack up her stuffed animals?"

Jimmy broke in. "I sure missed out on that scene. You had me leave the room when I could have met this weird lady myself."

"She might have thrown a fit," Lucy admonished. "She gets pretty excited sometimes."

"What did Mom think of her?"

"She fussed at her all the time, but I think she secretly loved having Sarah act as her private nurse," Lucy said.

"I guess we'll never understand the mystery of Sarah," Betsy said.

"I'm sure we won't. But some things are better when they're not fully understood," Lucy said. "We'll never know how Mom felt that night; nor will we ever know what part, if any, Sarah played."

Jimmy sighed deeply. "Doesn't this whole affair seem terribly ironic? Mom was apparently thinking that she was tired of living and then by some freak accident she actually does die. It's hard to believe that we came here for a birthday party and will end up going to a funeral."

"I know," Lucy agreed. "All we know for sure is that Mom choked on a Jordon almond."

CHAPTER 40

Sarah sat in her room holding Florry's panda trying to understand everything that happened. *Mrs. Jahnke said that Florry died and that she wasn't coming back.* That thought became more and more frightening as she worried over Florry's empty bed.

"I see your roommate has gone," Visitor said.

Sarah was startled to hear the familiar voice. She wasn't sure why he was there, unless he was angry with her. "Florry died," she said matter-of-factly.

"Yes, I know. She wanted to die."

"I'm so sorry," Sarah said smiling like an amused child.

Visitor frowned before walking over to the other bed and fingering the red rose. "Is this for your roommate?"

Sarah couldn't remember how to answer, so she pointed to the window. "Snow?"

"Do you like snow, Sarah?"

"Nooo. Snow is cold."

"Yes, of course." Visitor returned to the chair and asked, "Do you want to die?"

That word again. Once I wanted to die. She knew Visitor waited for an answer; she wanted to please him. "Thy Kingdom Come," she said with a winning smile and added, "Thy Will Be Done."

"That's very good, Sarah."

As soon as he left, the night that she wanted to die flashed before her with complete clarity of detail.

She opened her eyes and saw Jonathan carefully bathing her and tending to her bruised face. He seemed so loving and caring that she thought she must be dreaming. Jonathon was always so cold and distant. He was speaking quietly. "Who did this to you? You must tell me so I can call the police."

The words were frightening and she didn't want to answer. *Police? What did I do?* She shook her head and whispered, "I don't know."

Jonathan looked at her with such compassion and tenderness that she wondered why he was being so kind. "Someone attacked you. Do you know who it was?"

His words meant nothing to her. The only thing she felt was the terrible throbbing in her head and the pain that held her lower body captive. "I was at the library," she began softly, "and then —"

When she hesitated, he said, "It's okay. Don't try to talk right now. Ralph will be here soon."

Ralph is coming here? When the doorbell rang she could hear him talking to Jonathan. She could not make out the words but occasionally 'rape,' 'police,' and 'criminal' jarred her into thinking. She remembered locking the library door and the cleansing walk through the snow that felt so fresh and cool.

She liked their family doctor, Ralph Peterson but when he started his examination she thought he was unusually probing. It wasn't like him to be rough and once she cried out in pain. "I'm sorry, Sarah. I just want to make sure you'll be okay. You've had quite an ordeal. Can you talk about it?"

She had no idea what he meant and repeated the word, "Ordeal?"

"Can you tell me who hurt you?"

Try as she might, she could not answer and began to cry—long sobbing heaves with no tears. Every deep gasping breath she took was painful.

Doctor Peterson's hands were gentle as he took her arm and said, "I'll give you something for the pain," he said, "and it will help you sleep." She felt the prick of a needle and then nothing.

A few days later, she got a phone call. The voice was almost familiar. "Hi Sarah. This is Janice. How are you feeling?"

"Janice?"

"From the library. Jonathan told me you were ill."

She knew a Janice once. "Yes I was, but I'm better now."

"Will you be coming back to work soon? Folks are asking about you."

"Not right now," she said.

There was a pause before Janice continued. "I see. Well, I hope you get better. We're looking forward to seeing you again."

"Thank you."

When she hung up the phone, Visitor came into the room. She was terrified at the sight of a strange man and almost screamed for Jonathan.

Then, in the gentlest, most quieting voice he said, "Don't be frightened. I won't hurt you."

She looked into his eyes and knew he could be trusted. "Who are you?"

"I am your friend. I will call on you from time to time and protect you from harm."

Sarah felt a sense of comfort and well-being pervade her body. She would never be afraid again. "Thy Will Be Done," she said.

"Good. Good."

After Visitor came into her life and she allowed him to be her mentor, she saw no need to return to the library. *I want to be safe.*

CHHAPTER 41

A day after the funeral, Sarah was sitting quietly in her easy chair waiting for Florry to return. *She didn't die; I didn't die.* But every time she looked at the bed, it was still empty. The red rose turned brown so she dropped it into the wastebasket. *Dirty!*

Mrs. Jahnke came into her room. "Sarah? We have a nice lady who is going to move in with you," she said.

"Florry?" She was delighted to hear that she returned.

"No, I'm afraid it's not Florry. This woman's name is Rebecca. She's about your age and she's anxious to meet you."

"I see."

"One of the aide's will come with her belongings." She looked up and said, "Oh, there she is now."

Sarah watched the aide open Florry's drawers and fill them with personal items, watched while she opened the cupboard and began hanging clothing. "No!" *Didn't they know that Florry was coming back? Where would she put her animals and all her other things?*

"What's wrong, Sarah?" Mrs. Jahnke asked.

"Florry. I want Florry."

Mrs. Jahnke took her hand and sat beside her. She spoke soothingly. "Florry died. She won't be coming back. I'm sure you and Rebecca will become good friends."

"Nooo." *Florry will be mad.* Sarah stood and began removing the contents of all the drawers that the aide had just filled. "No!" she said emphatically.

Mrs. Jahnke and the aide stared at each other. Finally Mrs. Jahnke said, "Take Rebecca's things back to the office. We'll see if there's another way to solve this problem."

As soon as they left, Sarah made sure all the drawers and cupboard were empty and smiled. *I don't want to make Florry mad.* She went to her chair that faced the window and looked out at the spring-like day. There were a few brave crocuses peeping out of the ground in the commons area and the tree outside her window was beginning to bud. She looked down at her boots and removed them as well as her scarf. *No more snow*

***

Mrs. Jahnke talked to the doctor. "Sarah, in 103 refuses to let anyone move into her room. She has the idea that Florry will be returning."

"Is she going to be a problem?"

"You know that we have a waiting list. We have to fill the beds."

"I understand. What does she say?"

"Only that Florry will be back and then she proceeded to remove everything from the drawers and cupboard."

"I guess we'll have to give her something to make her less anxious. I'll prescribe a mild tranquilizer. That should do the trick. Let me know if she is more receptive."

"Thank you, Doctor."

***

The next day, Mrs. Jahnke and the aide returned to 103 and unpacked Rebecca's belongings. Sarah watched but said nothing. When Rebecca came into the room and was introduced, Sarah looked her over and shook her head. "Where's Florry?"

Mrs. Jahnke said, "Florry won't be coming right now. Rebecca will be staying here for a while. Okay?"

Sarah beamed. "Oookay."

Mrs. Jahnke breathed a sigh of relief and after making sure that Rebecca was settled, left the room.

***

Sarah knew that Florry was somewhere—maybe in the building, maybe outside. She would have to find her. With that in mind, she began a walking crusade. Every morning after breakfast, she made the rounds of the whole facility going into every room that was not locked. Sometimes she startled male patients in various states of undress and they ranted at her. These encounters were doubly frightening because they were men and also they were angry. She made note of these rooms and never went back.

The personnel were aware of Sarah's new behavior patterns and noticed how she entered a room with a hopeful look on her face and left the room disappointed. Her seeking expeditions became part of her morning activity and after a week or two, no one remarked on her comings and goings.

Sarah began to be fearful that Florry wasn't somewhere inside the facility and resolved to look outside the building. It was April and spring had come to Carson City. Sarah looked longingly at the budding trees and flowers outside her window and decided to go out. She got through the lobby and as far as the front entrance before a young woman stopped her.

"Where are you going, Sarah?"

"To find Florry."

"She isn't out there," the receptionist said gently.

"Oh, I see." She started to smile and then remembered to ask, "Where is Florry?"

"She won't be coming back. Let's go to your room, okay?"

Sarah allowed herself to be guided back to 103. *Maybe Florry's there.*

Her roommate was lying on the bed and for a moment, Sarah thought that Florry had returned. She walked to the bed, looked down and began to cry.

The receptionist rang the call button and soon an aide was at her side. "What's wrong?" she asked.

"Florry?"

"She's gone. Rebecca is your friend, now." The aide said comforting words but Sarah wasn't listening. She began to understand that perhaps what they were telling her was the truth. But the thought of Florry never returning seemed incomprehensible. *Where did she go?*

When the aide left, Sarah laid on the bed and felt utterly alone. *Everyone's gone. Except me.*

From that day, Sarah began to have periods of time when she sat and stared out the window. The aides noticed that she no longer played cards or read from her Watchtower book. Her exercise time—two o'clock—came and went without her taking advantage of her regimen, but perhaps the most striking change was that she made no effort to look smart and tidy. Her hair, always pulled up into a chignon, now hung loose and stringy and she was often seen wearing mismatched clothing. The nurses and aides knew she was grieving and tried to help by having friendly chats and suggesting new interests. Sarah listened, not hearing and continued to wait.

CHAPTER 42

Two weeks after the funeral, Lucy had not yet accepted the fact that her mother's well-being was no longer her responsibility. She found herself buying items that she knew Florry needed before realizing that her mother was gone. On these occasions, she apologized to the check-out clerks and returned the merchandize. She found herself thinking of things she would tell her mother the next time she saw her; she got in the car several times with the express purpose of driving to the facility. She wondered if Sarah was having the same problems accepting the void in her life.

The following Saturday she drove to Carson City to see Sarah. Before she went into the room she stopped at the nurses' station and inquired. What she heard was disturbing. "I'm afraid that Sarah is slipping into a depressive state. She's not the Sarah that you knew a few weeks ago. Besides the obvious changes that I'm sure you will see, she also does not eat as well as she once did. She takes a bite or two of food and then pushes it away saying she's full."

"How awful. Maybe I can do something—talk to her and see if I can cheer her up."

"We'd appreciate any help you can give us. As you know she has no family."

"I know." Lucy felt a pang of grief as she realized that she too, was almost without family. *It's only me and Jimmy, now.*

She went down the hall to the familiar room and was afraid that she'd not be able to go inside. Then swallowing her fears and trying to think of Sarah, she walked in. Her mother's bed was occupied by a stranger and the sight of someone else in *her mother's bed* was unnerving. She took a deep breath and said, "Good morning Ladies," and looked for Sarah in the other bed.

"Where's Sarah?" she asked. The woman in her mother's bed pointed. "Right there, can't you see her?"

Lucy was appalled at what was supposed to be Sarah. The once youthful looking eighty-year-old woman had the appearance of a thin, emaciated old lady—disheveled and worn. *How could she change this much in just three weeks?* "Sarah?"

"My name is Sarah," the woman said, but the beautiful, winning smile was gone. She looked at Lucy carefully and seemed to recognize her, then shook her head.

"Do you remember me, Sarah? I'm Lucy."

A dim light of recollection appeared in her eyes, to be replaced by a cloud of confusion. "Nooo."

"I'm Florry's daughter. Remember her?"

"Where's Florry?" she asked expectantly.

"She's gone, but I came to see you."

"I see." She continued to stare at Lucy and the sight of the once vibrant woman was more than Lucy could bear.

Lucy began crying—soft tears that she knew were for Sarah and for her mother and for herself. *How can I help this lady?* She had to get out of the room, so she said, "Let's go for a little walk, Sarah."

Sarah got up from her bed, clasped her panda and took Lucy's hand. She looked up expectantly and Lucy wondered if she thought they were going to see Florry. "We'll walk around the building," she said.

Sarah immediately perked up and moved briskly out the door and into the hall. She entered every room, checking on the occupants while Lucy waited, not understanding. When they reached the nurses' station, Lucy stopped and raised an eyebrow. The nurse on duty whispered, "She makes rounds every morning. She's looking for Florry."

This bit of information so moved Lucy that she knew she had to leave. "Let's go back to your room. I have to go to work," she said. After hastily guiding Sarah to 103, she left after stopping for a minute at the station.

"I can't stay now," she said wiping her eyes. "But I do want you to call me regarding Sarah. I can come back to see her every few days."

"That would be wonderful," the nurse said. "We'll keep in touch."

"Thanks."

CHAPTER 43

Sarah got progressively worse. Every time that Lucy came to visit she seemed more and more detached. She still did not recognize Lucy, but there were times that a spark of remembrance gave Lucy hope.

May was a beautiful month that year and now when Lucy visited, she took Sarah outside to the gardens. They sat in the sunshine, hand in hand—each locked in memories from the past. Lucy thought that Sarah looked especially vulnerable that day. Her skin had taken on a transparency and she was so thin and frail that Lucy knew she must be near death. She was a wisp of her former self and rarely spoke in the disarming way she had. Occasionally she smiled at Lucy, but said nothing.

Every time that Lucy visited, she brought a small gift—a flower or candy or a little stuffed animal. The gifts were accepted—Sarah remembered to say thank you—but soon set aside and ignored. Lucy noticed that her mother's panda was still Sarah's constant companion. She took it everywhere.

When Lucy walked Sarah back to her room, she sensed that Sarah was acting more like her old self. And when they sat facing each other, Sarah's face lit up in total recognition. "Lucy?" she said.

"I'm Lucy. Do you remember me?"

"I'm Sarah," she said proudly.

"I know. So how are you today, Sarah?"

"Thy Will Be Done," she replied in the way that was once so familiar.

Then, as though she suddenly thought of something, she rose from the chair and went to her bedside table. When she pulled open the drawer, Lucy was astonished at the disarray. Scraps of paper, loose playing cards and personal items littered the drawer. There were two books amid the clutter. One was Sarah's Watchtower; the other was the notebook that Lucy had seen several times. Sarah removed the notebook and handed it to Lucy. She offered it as though it was a sacred object and simply said, "For you."

Lucy started to open it. The cover had no title, but Sarah exclaimed, "No! For you."

"You want me to take it home?"

Sarah nodded and when Lucy slipped the book into her handbag, Sarah smiled. "I'm so sorry," she said. Then she got into her bed and let Lucy pull up the coverlet.

"I'll be back, Sarah. Take care."

***

Visitor came as soon as Lucy left and sat in a chair near her bed. "You gave her Jonathan's journal, I see."

"Oookay." *Was he angry?*

"How long have you kept it?"

She didn't understand his question. "Thy Will Be Done," she said looking at him intently.

"You won't need it anymore," he said with a faint smile of approval.

"I see." She wondered why he came and said, "It's going to rain."

"Probably not, Sarah. I came to take you with me. Are you ready?"

He was going to take her to Florry. She knew it. "Florry?" she asked. "Where's Florry?"

"She's waiting for you."

"I'm so sorry," she said, delighted to hear his words.

"It won't be long now," he said and left.

CHAPTER 44

Lucy could hardly wait until she got home to open the well worn notebook, brown-edged with age. The first page identified the writer and his address. A small sheet of note paper had been attached to this page with transparent tape. The note appeared to be a later addition.

JONATHAN COOPERS
1411 MAPLEHURST STREET,
CARSON CITY, WISCONSIN.

I began this journal in January 1979 after my wife Sarah suffered a horrible crime against her person. Most of this journal describes our daily lives from that day until the present. Recently I decided to summarize Sarah's life and her condition. The last few pages of this notebook contain that information.

In August of 1989 my doctor told me that I had six months—perhaps a year to live. I made financial arrangements for Sarah so that she will want for nothing in her old age. My attorney, Arthur Whittley, has all the necessary documents. Since neither of us has family, she will live at the Carson County Care Center upon my death.

I have instructed Sarah to keep this book with her at all times and I trust that she will honor my wish.

Lucy was astounded. *Sarah had this with her all these years and no one ever read it.* Lucy recalled the times that Sarah seemed to be reading Watchtower. *I'll bet she wasn't even reading. She either can't or won't read. How odd!*

Curiosity got the best of her and she began to leaf through the pages. Most of the entries were quite short—sometimes telling an anecdote about Sarah, other times telling what Jonathan did for her.

She noticed various doctor's names and their guarded prognoses. As far as she could tell it was an ordinary diary and she promised herself that she would read it in its entirety. But now the driving need to understand Sarah made her turn to the back pages.

"It is August, 1990 and the six months to a year that my doctors' awarded me have come to an end. I have thought about this summary for a long time; I want to write about Sarah.

That night she came home half dead and so cold I was afraid she was suffering from hypothermia. I carried her into the house and laid her on the bed. Before I did anything I called Ralph our family doctor, and he agreed to come. I immediately got warm water and cloths and blankets and proceeded to wash her soiled and bruised body. She remained unconscious for a time and then awakened and recognized me. I knew what had happened to her—there was enough blood and bruising—but she seemed to have blocked the scene from her mind.

If she had told me who did this to her, I'm sure I would have killed him. I wanted to call the police but she seemed to have no recollection of what happened. She mumbled that she locked the door of the library and walked home in the snow. When the doctor came and examined her, he said that I should be relieved because her body would heal. He urged me to call the police and I told him I would. I never did.

The library director called a couple of days later but apparently Sarah said she would not return to work. I didn't press her, thinking she needed time to forget the incident. When several weeks went by without Sarah offering any information—she always repeated the same story, 'I locked the door and walked home in the snow.'—I took her to another doctor. He found nothing physically wrong with her. But I could see that her personality was changing.

She developed a need for spic and span order in our house. Sarah was always a good housekeeper—now she became obsessive about cleanliness. I worried about her not having enough to occupy herself. I brought books home, but she would typically open the cover, look at the title page and close the book. She became reluctant to leave the house. At first I accompanied her on shopping trips, but even then she acted like a frightened child when she saw strangers—especially men.

She trusted me, but from the time she collapsed on the front steps, she never allowed me to touch her and refused my advances. After six months of this behavior I made an appointment with a psycho-therapist. 'Sarah may never consciously recall her ordeal,' I was told. 'She has closed her mind to decision-making and skills that she may have had. She will avoid anything or anyone that in some way makes her think of her experience. She's happy and content in this little world of her own making and will come out only when she's ready.' Those words confirmed what I already suspected.

I considered it my obligation as her husband to make life as easy for her as possible. Over the years, our marriage had become one of convenience but I vowed to attend to her needs as any loving husband should do. I knew that she wrote poetry so once I had the idea that she might want to resume that pastime. I searched her drawers and closets and found nothing. In desperation I emptied her purse and found a key and assumed it was for a safety deposit box. Forging her signature I went to the bank and found that she had several books of poems. These I brought home, thinking to jar her memory. She looked at them as though she had never seen them. After leafing through the pages she looked at me with a questioning expression. "What are these?"

As the months and years went by, she spoke fewer and fewer words and began to answer questions with wildly confusing answers. I watched this regression with a sad heart, but had no way of reaching her. We lived this way for eleven years. She never got any better.

Now, as I look back over that time I blame myself for her condition. I shouldn't have allowed her to live as a protected child without expecting anything from her. I never commented on her obvious breaks with reality. In short, I feel guilty for not having done more to return her to a normal life."

Lucy put the book down and stared at it. *What a strange story. Sarah was a poet? She almost always spoke in monosyllables.*

EPILOGUE

It was beginning to get dark when Lucy finished reading the journal. The more she thought about Sarah and her life, the more depressed she became. *Surely there's something I can do for her.* And then suddenly, like an insight so obvious as to be ludicrous, she understood why Sarah gave her the book. *She's going to die!*

Her first impulse was to call the facility. *What shall I tell them? That Sarah gave me her husband's journal? They might not find that suspect.* She grabbed her car keys and drove to Carson City, rushed into the facility and went to 103. Her mother's old bed was occupied; Sarah's bed was neatly made and a red rose lay on the pillow.

ABOUT THE AUTHOR

Caro Somers calls Newport, Oregon 'home.' She is not a native, but when walking on the ocean beaches, she wishes she were. Her books reflect her interest in the arts; she taught Humanities in a Michigan Community College for nineteen years.

Caro writes about people – their dreams, aspirations, relationships and tragedies – from her own experiences in this country and abroad. Her life is rich with three children from a former marriage and one grandson. She and her husband EJ Warren, enjoy the coastal surroundings, travel and retirement.

Her novels include:

THE LAST BUS TO HILLERY
COUSINS' FIVE
WHEN WE REACH SEPTEMBER
CLARA'S HOUSE
THE BRIDGE
ANGELINA
FROM OUT OF THE DEPTHS
ARIEL
TALK TO ME
NO GREATER LOVE.